WHITE BIZANGO

WHITE BIZANGO
Stephen Gallagher

THE BROOLIGAN PRESS
LONDON
NEW YORK

First published in Great Britain 2002 by PS Publishing LLP, in hardcover and paperback

This edition published 2017 by The Brooligan Press
Rights and Permissions: Howard Morhaim Literary Agency
30 Pierrepont St, Brooklyn NY 11201

ISBN: 0 9957973 8 2
ISBN-13: 978 0 9957973 8 3

With special thanks to Michael Chafetz, PhD, ABPP
I owe you another, Catahoula Mike

.

THAT OLE GALLAGHER VOODOO-HOODOO BE COOKIN'

JOE R LANSDALE

FIRST BOOK I read by Stephen Gallagher was *Valley of Lights*. Blew me away. I knew that the writer was British writing about the US, but that feeling didn't last long. I was soon absorbed in the story.

I wasn't the only one blown away by *Valley of Lights*. In fact, that novel gave Gallagher his name here in the States, made him a writer of prominence. I know I was impressed, and was more than a little proud to share a *Night Visions* anthology with him some years later.

I think I wrote better material because I knew Stephen Gallagher was going to be in the anthology with me, and I didn't want to look like a goober beside him, though I may have anyway.

A goober standing beside Stephen Gallagher may not be an image you want in your head, so we'll just let that one lie and move on.

One thing I especially liked about *Valley of Lights*, and for that matter everything I've read since by Gallagher, is his style. He writes with a rhythm.

My guess is he can't actually write a story or novel until he feels this rhythm in his head. Which is not to suggest he's dancing around his work room to the inner drums and rhythm guitars inside his skull, though that's highly possible, but his work has that kind of beat and boogie that only writers of character and style have. He plots well. But his strength is in the purity of his story-telling and in the development of his characters, and these are out-growths of, well, The Storyteller's Boogie, and only a true story teller can do it. It's a kind of mental mating dance by which the writer seduces the reader and they can still feel good about themselves in the morning.

Stephen Gallagher can also take a pretty regular idea and just plain old beat the tar out of it, remold it, and make it something unusual, totally unexpected, and riveting.

Which brings us to the novel at hand.

First off, *White Bizango* is written in the first person. My favourite form of storytelling. It has an immediacy, as well as an intimacy, that I enjoy. When I was a kid I read a novel by Edgar Rice Burroughs, (*A Princess of Mars*) written in first person, and it was so convincing that somewhere, deep inside of me, I truly believed the story, and from that time on I have preferred this approach.

Burroughs was a master storyteller, but not a master stylist.

As I have already pointed out, Stephen Gallagher is both. This book is so easy to read, so riveting, that you are briskly pulled into the story. I have to say it again. Man, this book is easy to read, and it's wonderful. Its seemingly simple approach belies its true complexity.

Here Gallagher has captured the taste and feel of Louisiana in a style that can only be called American, and he has also written the best book of his career. It's short and swift. A small package. But as they say, dynamite comes in small packages.

Here's a box of it now.

Did I say this is the best novel of his career?

Okay. I might have missed one of his novels, maybe two, but this one made the hair on the back of my neck stand up.

White Bizango's mood wraps around you like a warm blanket. Gave me the kind of sensation I used to have as a kid, watching some monster movie late at night, rainy and windy outside, sitting on the couch, or in front of it, tenting a blanket over me, feeling wonderfully and pleasantly terrified.

How to describe it further without giving away its prizes?

Fast paced?

Oh, yeah. That's good.

Rich and evocative of location?

That works, big time.

Pumping with the rich warm blood of a true storyteller?

Said that already, but it bears repeating.

Got that voodoo-hoodoo going?

You betcha. Classic voodoo stuff. But kicked in the ass by Gallagher to give it a feel reminiscent of voodoo stories and films you may have encountered, but, somehow . . . different.

But is it creepy?

Yeah. Creepy, folks. Real damn creepy. Old style creepy. A kind of creepy you don't get much anymore in books or films. And, I think I should point out, this would make a great film. A real chilly-billy of a deal. Best read late at night, when the day's concerns are past, but just before you get too tired, and if you are tired, you won't be long. This dude will hook you and drag you along and keep you awake better than a shot of caffeine.

What else?

Oh, I know. The most important thing of all.

It's as readable as they come.

So, let's cut to the chase.

Quit screwing around. I'm just getting in the way, gushing all over the place. So quit listening to me.

I'll shut up now. And if I don't, push me aside.

It's time to start reading.

Joe R Lansdale
July 2002

WHITE BIZANGO

Bizango: A secret society of practitioners who operate outside of accepted vodoun practice, often performing harmful services for their clients in exchange for payment. Using various techniques that include natural poisons, hallucinogens and psychological conditioning through ritual, these individuals are largely responsible for the public misconception of vodoun as a religion of supernatural evil.

Christopher Speaks: American Voodoo and the Modern Mind
Carolina Chapter House Press, 1987

Practising magic to get what you want is like laughing at the TV to make Frasier come on.

Abraham Shapiro, IPD

ONE

NOBODY SHOPS on Row Street any more. For that we have the Iberville Mall, out between the town and the lake. It's our civic showpiece. They built it on land where the battery works used to be.

Amy had taken the car, so I was driving the Jeep. In the Detective Division we use our own vehicles and claim mileage. Missing child reports don't often get passed to us from the mall; in most cases their own security people resolve the situation. Usually it's just a matter of the child going astray, or hiding from its parents out of mischief or pique.

But unless he'd been found since I took the call, this child had been gone for almost an hour. That made it more serious. As I came in on the perimeter road, I couldn't see anyone searching the parking lot; they should have been securing it by now, but all I could see were a couple of our cruisers by the main entrance and a small crowd outside.

I turned in at the first opening and cut across the empty asphalt. They were supposed to have cleaned up the ground before they laid it, although I've been told there are cracks that leak a kind of orange goo when the water table rises.

Iberville, West Louisiana. Some parts of it aren't too pretty, but it's home.

I parked and went over. To the officer on the doors I said, "Did the boy turn up yet?"

"They're looking at tape in the store," he said, and told me where to aim for.

It had the usual interior arrangement—one of every-thing, a food court, multiple sportswear shops and a Sunglasses Hut. One end of the complex was dominated by an upmarket department store where people went to look at the expensive brands before buying copies elsewhere. The store had entrances on both levels, and it aspired to class. It was the smart place to register your wedding list and its coffee shop was the choice of the ladies who lunch.

The mall would have been quiet at this hour anyway, but thanks to the security operation it was almost deserted. Some of the salespeople had emerged from their units and were chatting in the concourse, arms folded, eyes wary, ready to head back to their posts at the first sign of a return to commerce.

The department store had no doors, just a wide walk-in entrance. From the greeter I got directions to the customer service desk on the upper floor, where a woman was waiting. Someone had brought her a chair, but she was standing. They'd assigned a young sales associate to look after her and I think she'd been looking for someone bigger to get her teeth into.

Well, I suppose that's unfair. But when she sensed my approach and turned to face me, the look in her eyes was one of readiness to attack. I thought about how I'd feel if I was in the same position over one of my daughters. We'd lost one of them for a few minutes in a branch of The Gap, once. Aged five, she'd sidestepped into the middle of a rack of jeans and stayed there to enjoy our panic.

"My name's John Lafcadio," I said. "I'm a detective. Are you Mrs Boudreaux?"

She got straight to it.

"My son's been kidnapped," she said.

"I understand he's missing," I said, "but what makes

you think he's been taken?"

"I'm certain of it," she said. "He knows the dangers. He wouldn't walk away."

I looked around for someone in authority; but there was only the sales associate, a short-haired, brown-eyed girl who looked like an eager child in a grownup's uniform. I said to the woman, "I need to ask you a couple of things. Do you live with your son's father?"

"Of course I do." Then she checked herself, as if there was something she'd forgotten for a moment. "Well, it's more complicated than that."

"Meaning what?"

"We're not separated, but he's hospitalized. Kenny is not the man who took my son. There are no custody issues here, Detective Lafcadio. Please don't waste your energy in that direction."

"Nine times out of ten we find the child and they've just wandered off and got themselves lost."

"And one time in ten you find what?"

For which I didn't have a ready answer.

She was in her early thirties (thirty-two, I later learned), with cold blue eyes and blonde hair in a precise, expensive cut. If it was a dye job, it was one of the best I've ever seen. A tad skinnier than was good for her, making her shoulders look bony and square but giving her the kind of dress-up-doll figure that gay couturiers love.

I said, "Have you received any kind of a threat that leads you to think someone's taken your son, Mrs Boudreaux?"

She spoke across me. "Someone was talking about closing down the mall and letting nobody out. Has that been done yet?"

"We've got people watching all the exits."

"That won't stop him!"

"Stop who, Mrs Boudreaux?"

She checked herself, and took a moment to choose her words.

"Whoever it was that took Christopher," she said.

So there was some kind of a backstory that she was determined not to give me. It would have to be drawn from her eventually, but there were a few more immediate things that I needed to do. I asked the associate about their security tapes, and she told me how to find the office where they kept the machines. She said that the manager was checking them now.

Julie Boudreaux said, "I want to see the tapes."

"I need you to hold on here a while longer," I said. "I'll send for you if there's anything to see."

She still wanted to go with me, but I managed to get her to stay on the sales floor while I went off to talk to the store manager.

"WE JUST found it," the manager's deputy said. She was a young woman with dark red hair in gel spikes, and eyes that gave you the feeling they rarely saw daylight.

"How does it look?" I said.

And the manager himself said, "Not good."

They rewound the tape and played it back for me.

We were in a windowless office suite, backstage behind the crystal ware section. The two of them were reviewing the morning's images on an cheap-looking portable TV set with a built-in video slot under the screen, the kind you usually see out on the sales floor running infomercials about kitchen appliances.

The associate must have called ahead, because they'd been expecting me when I arrived.

The screen was divided into four. Their surveillance wasn't state-of-the-art, but one of those systems taking single frames every second or so. There's no sound and the quality's not great, but you can get several days' worth of sampled activity onto the one tape.

The deputy pointed to the top left-hand quadrant of the screen. The timecode showed today's date and a time of 10.03.

There they were. A boy and his mother. The boy was fair-haired and aged around nine or ten, but you couldn't say much more about him than that. His mother was on the edge of the screen and in two frames had left it completely, so the boy was on his own.

Suddenly a man was there with him.

You didn't see him walk in, he just appeared. This was like a drama where the story was all in the missed moments and you had to fill in the gaps for yourself. Three still frames of conversation and then they were walking out together, in the opposite direction from the woman. At no time did the man face the camera. In one shot, his hand was on the boy's shoulder.

They knew each other. Had to. Nothing else made sense.

I said, "How long before the mother raised the alarm?"

"Seconds," the manager said. "See for yourself."

There she was, onscreen again, looking for her son in the aisle where she'd seen him last. Now she was spinning in panic, now she was flying out in a blur. I glanced at the other angles on the screen and in one of them I thought I saw what might have been the man and boy crossing a different part of the floor together, but I don't know. At that resolution it could have been anyone.

I said, "And how long before you started your missing child protocol?"

"Just as long as it took us to get a description from her," the manager said. "Three, four minutes. No more."

His deputy said, "The way she acted, it was almost like she'd been expecting it to happen."

"That's not an appropriate speculation," her employer said sharply. "Keep it to yourself, please, Jill."

"Sorry."

I said, "I'm going to call my boss and tell him we need a team out here. Where's Mall Security based?"

Spike-haired Jill, slightly chastened by her reprimand, was assigned to take me there.

This meant leaving the store, crossing the hall by the fountain and the central bank of escalators, and waiting to be buzzed through into another behind-the-scenes stairway down at the far end of a rest room corridor. She was subdued, and said very little.

"Got any more inappropriate speculation for me?" I said as we waited to be let in.

"I'm sorry about that. I spoke out of turn," she said. Out here where the light was better, I could see that her night-owl look was mainly due to the combination of a pale complexion and heavy eyeliner. I'd estimate she wasn't much more than twenty years old.

"I'm not putting you down," I said. "I'll take any idea that's going."

"It really did happen as fast as he said. It's not the greatest place to work but I won't criticise the people. There would have been someone on every door within five minutes. Police callout after another ten when the boy wasn't found."

"And how long to walk out of there? Less than two?"

"Two at the most. Depending on which exit you made for."

Stable doors, and bolting horses.

The door clicked open and she left me to descend the stairs on my own. I'd never been in this part of the complex before.

Down here it was no-frills, bare and functional, with painted cinderblock walls and exposed ducting. I could hear fans running somewhere, but the stairway felt airless and warm. I could feel myself breaking into a light sweat as I reached the door to the security suite and pushed my way in.

It was cooler in here. Lots of screens, lots of phones. Three men in uniform and a radio console with tags hanging on a hook board above it, each tag representing a guard on duty. One was scanning the real-time screens, another appeared to be reviewing the entire morning's recordings on fast playback. The third man swung his chair around to get a look at me.

I knew Bill Stevens from when he'd retired and gone to run site security for Colonial Sugar, but he didn't appear to remember me. He said he did, but the recognition wasn't there in his eyes. No matter. It had been ten years at least, and I'd been in uniform then. He'd lost a significant amount of weight, and I wondered what had caused it.

He said, "We've got four main entrances and they're all covered. At first we just stopped anyone we saw leaving with a child. Now we're more or less in lockdown. I believe there's a good chance they're still somewhere inside the building."

"What about other ways out?"

"Deliveries come in by a network of tunnels down on this level. It's like Disneyland, you never see the trucks come and go. Each store has its own numbered loading bay and each store's responsible for controlling access to it from above."

"Controlling it how?"

"Keys or swipe cards or keypad codes. You name it.

Everyone has their own system."

"What if there's one sloppy joe who won't play the game right?"

"We still control the gates where the trucks enter and leave."

I looked over the shoulder of the man who was watching the screens. Some of them showed those delivery tunnels, and two showed the parking lot outside.

I said to Bill, "And how good are your people?"

"On the budget they give me? Most are okay, but some of them . . . " He glanced around and lowered his voice, but not by much. "To call them pond life would be an insult to bacteria." He indicated the screen that showed the western side of the lot. "Your cavalry's here," he said.

And he was right. Four cars converging, all detectives pulled from other jobs and reassigned.

I went up to meet them and to tell them what I'd found so far.

TWO

YOU MUST have heard this one. A child goes missing. Sometimes it's in a shopping center, sometimes at the beach or in an amusement park. The alarm is raised and the staff respond with surprising speed, following a well-drilled protocol that has all the exits covered in minutes or less. The child is then found quickly; drugged and abandoned by its kidnapper, usually in a bathroom cubicle or the changing rooms. If it's a boy, he's been put into a dress and there's a wig lying somewhere close to hand. If a girl, her distinctive long hair has been partially hacked off. In some versions they're being walked out of the building in a disguise when the parent spots them by recognizing their shoes.

It's one of the classic urban myths. Only one element of it happens to be true, and that's the existence of a protocol. Sometimes it's called a Code Adam, named for a boy murdered in Florida in 1981. Not every store follows it, but this one had. I hoped that Bill Stevens was right and that there was a fair chance that Christopher Boudreaux might still be within the mall somewhere, but I had my doubts. They're such big, sprawling places, with too many ways in and out and too few people controlling the access.

I met my boss and the others by the fountain, which had water running down a slate rock face into a pool surrounded by exotic plants. Glass-sided elevators rose and fell while hidden speakers played birdsong. Strange, strange, strange. Outside these walls, the surrounding terrain resembled dead paddy fields and the only song was that of the distant truck horn.

My boss was Major Bob Lambert, silver-haired and pugnacious-looking, usually seen around the office with his reading glasses on top of his head. He listened to what I'd learned, and to my certainty that I'd been given less than the full story.

"So where does she say the father is?" he asked.

"Hospitalized, she says."

"Did she say where and for what?"

"It was a struggle to get that much out of her."

"Find out. Can you do that for me, John? There are hospitals and there are hospitals. I'd like to know what kind he's in and how close an eye they're keeping on him."

He gave Jimmie Noone the job of organizing roadblocks, and told Wade Bourgeois to arrange a parking lot search while everyone else concentrated on a top-to-tail of the mall complex itself. I went and sat in the empty food court for the five minutes it took me to call the office and set one of the civilian workers on the search for Kenny Boudreaux and the nature of his delicate condition. Then I went back to the store.

I could hear Julie Boudreaux from the other end of the sales floor. Bob Lambert was getting the blasting that she'd been working up to with me, and I didn't envy him for it.

I've already told this three times . . . I heard her saying. *For God's sake how many more . . .*

I made my way across the floor to the spot from which Christopher Boudreaux had been taken. It was by the lingerie aisle. I never know where to look in those places. The way they display all that sexy underwear on headless, limbless torsos, it's like they invited Henry Lee Lucas to design himself a theme park.

I already had a rough idea of the direction they'd taken. My thinking was that they'd have headed straight for the nearest exit and been out of there even before the Code Adam was called. From what I'd seen it had been that quick, that purposeful. Downstairs there were doors leading directly into the parking lot, but those would have taken longer to reach. For speed they could only have gone out onto the mall's upper level.

A junior manager in a white shirt and dark necktie was standing by what I reckoned to be the most likely exit. He had a pleasant smile and plague-of-boils skin.

I asked him, "Does this door get watched all the time?"

"Only when we're busy at weekends," he said, "or if there's a special reason like now."

"So if the child was brought out this way, you wouldn't be here to see it."

"Not if it happened before the staff call. But I can tell you it hasn't happened since. I've been here all the time."

I went out into the mall and looked around. Country music was playing softly, seeming to come from nowhere. Daylight came down from tinted glass panels high above. This was the closest we were going to get to the domed cities we'd been promised in the story magazines of my childhood. They weren't domed and they weren't half as exciting as they'd seemed back then, either.

This was a quiet side-spur of the mall, where at least half of the units hadn't even bothered to open for business this morning. Their internal lights were out, their shutters down. Only one was trading, a furniture store. Its entrance was almost directly opposite. I crossed and went inside.

It was a modern-looking showroom for third-world chic. Imagine the kind of furniture that would have been taken upriver into the tropical jungles by nineteenth-century planters, and then imagine that same furniture copied by cheap labor working on crude logs with nifty axes. There was a lot of recycled Indonesian hardwood and beaten brass; it looked like a prop store for The Swiss Family Robinson. And birdcages. Impractical birdcages everywhere, like painted wire pagodas.

What I didn't see was a sales assistant, nor did anybody appear until a good half-minute after I'd stood in the middle of the place and called out for one.

He had a slight stoop and long forearms, and he made me think of a mantis. I asked him if there was a way to the outside other than the main door, and he didn't understand me.

So I said, "Where would I have to go to meet a delivery truck?" and he led me into the back.

The first thing that I noted was that the sales floor was separated from the service areas by a two-inch door with a chrome deadbolt that even a gunshot wouldn't dent. It was operated by a state-of-the-art keypad lock, a five-digit model that could neither be hacked nor picked in a hurry. It represented the highest grade of security. Or it would, had the door not been propped open with a fire extinguisher.

"How long's this been like this?" I said.

The mantis shrugged.

"That's the way it always is," he said. "It gets awfully sticky down below."

Down below proved to be a complex of storerooms and office space lit only by fluorescent tubes and yes, he was right, the atmosphere was not the best. There was one big room for stock, a smaller room for packing up outgoing deliveries, and a corridor between them leading to staff quarters. By the stockroom was a freight elevator and alongside the elevator was an arrow pointing off to an emergency stairway in some other part of the area. I was taking an interest in this when I saw a man swing into sight at the corridor's far end. He was heading for one of the doorways but then he registered me and swung right around again to head back the way that he'd come.

"Sir?" I said, and he affected not to hear me. Carried right on and out of sight.

"Who was that?" I said to the mantis as I started to move after him, but the mantis didn't know.

"Not one of ours," he said.

Halfway down the corridor I stopped and pushed open the door that the man appeared to have been heading for.

The room was dark. I felt for the lightswitch and the overhead tube ginked into life.

This was where they kept all the store's broken and ex-display pieces. There was timber and bamboo and chickenwire, along with two carved elephants and one fair-haired ten-year-old boy, sitting on the floor between them with his arms around his knees.

He looked up at me and squinted against the light.

I was already reaching for my gun, checking it by touch under my coat. I said, "Are you Christopher?" and he nodded.

I said, "Why are you hiding?"

"Because he told me to," Christopher said.

He wasn't tied up, he wasn't drugged, and he didn't look as if he'd been manhandled or otherwise harmed. I stepped back out into the corridor and said to the mantis, "Get on your house phone to security, tell them to get the police down here. Tell them boy found, officer in pursuit. Can you remember that?"

"Boy found, officer in pursuit."

"And tell them that I think the suspect is aiming for the loading bays. Again?"

"I know some people think I look funny, but I'm not retarded," he said. "If you're going, you'd better go."

*   *   *

THERE WAS only one way he could have gone. Down a corridor that was like an internal back alley, where various businesses put out their trash in wheeled plastic dumpsters and the dumpsters were overflowing. While it was possible that he might have dodged through a doorway and back into the mall through another store, I didn't think it likely. I straight-armed some of the doors in passing, but they were rock-solid and bolted from the other side.

I tried to listen for him running, but these were the guts of the building and the guts were far from silent. The passageways echoed with the sounds of big engines and the whisper of dry air.

He had an escape route planned, was my guess. Taking the guesswork further, it was a route that he'd had to devise in a hurry; otherwise, why the need to park the boy in a quiet spot and come back for him? I reckoned that the original idea had been simply to walk him out of the mall in the same way that they'd walked out of the department store, but the speed of the lockdown had taken him by surprise.

The corridor ended in a waste elevator big enough to take about a dozen of the dumpsters. The cage front was shut and the cables in the shaft beyond it weren't moving, but the fire door to the adjoining stairway was still easing itself closed. Those hydraulic springs; you can't rush them and they're a great giveaway.

Instead of the stairwell I was expecting, I came out onto a high platform with a guardrail. This was a big, empty space under the mall, a couple of stories deep. I risked a look over the rail and saw a car directly below me.

It was a red Mazda with its engine running and its trunk popped open a few inches, probably intended to receive the boy and get him through the roadblocks. But the kidnapper had abandoned all that. Once he knew I'd seen him, he'd cut and run. Now he was down there. He had the driver's door open, and he was getting in behind the wheel.

I soon put a stop to that. I emptied half a dozen bullets into the hood and saw him bounce straight out again like a priest out of a bedroom window. I reloaded on my way down the stairs and gave chase when I hit the basement level.

Under other circumstances I'd have stopped and taken more note of my surroundings. I'd walked through the mall a hundred times but I'd never imagined any of this existing under my feet. It was like a pressed blank of an entire city street underground, no storefronts or windows, but cast-concrete walls and yellow sodium lights on the roof overhead. There were side-bays and loading platforms all down one side. Ahead was an intersection, red-light controlled like any normal crossing.

My man was about fifty yards ahead of me and, fortunately, he was no great athlete. He scrambled around the corner like a cow on rollerblades. I could hear something beeping, but I couldn't see what until I rounded the corner behind him.

Over us loomed the Godzilla-jawed rear end of a garbage truck, a massive, mega-bargain-bucket example of the species backing toward us down a big ramp. The ramp angled up toward daylight and the outside world. The truck was inching slowly because it all but filled the concrete tunnel from wall to wall. A miscalculation at the wheel would have meant big sparks and some serious structural damage. He'd even had to fold in his side-mirrors, and was reversing blind.

This was going to be interesting, because the fit was so tight that from here it looked as if there was no room for a body to get up along either side of the vehicle. Maybe at a squeeze, but I wouldn't have risked it. I didn't want to end up as so much mechanically-retrieved meat on the sharp edges of the bodywork.

My man seemed to reach the same conclusion. As he reached the truck, I saw him dive to the ground and start to crawl under.

I was about a dozen yards behind him. I could follow or I could let him go, banking on Bob Lambert or some of the others to be waiting for him when he popped out on the other side. But not much time had passed since I'd sent mantis-man off with the message. What were the chances of them being in the right place already? Not great. As detectives, we can be issued with radios but we mostly keep in base contact by phone. The others were probably being paged around now.

Shooting a fleeing felon is not a legal option, unfortunately. Even if it had been, I'd only ever shot at car tires in the line of duty. As I got to the truck, I dropped down on my haunches and looked underneath.

There he was, flat to the concrete and wriggling away from me, hugging the ground with the big greasy transmission shaft turning only inches above him.

"Hey!" I shouted over the engine noise and the warning beeps, half-hoping that his head would come up and there'd be a sudden brain-meat display when his skull met the shaft. Instant justice, and a lot less paperwork. But he didn't respond, unless it was to put more energy into that worming motion. He was moving like one of those battery-operated crawling soldiers, the ones with the Jack Kirby legs.

I saw that, if I was quick about it, I could grab one of those ankles and he'd be completely screwed. All I'd need to do would be to hang on until the truck had passed over, and then I could make the arrest.

By the time I'd thought about the suit I was wearing, I was already on the ground and crawling after him.

I regretted it almost immediately, but by now I was committed. The noise was deafening, and the sense of all that tonnage just above me was enough to make me want to freeze and hug the ground with my eyes shut until it had all gone by. I found that I couldn't judge the overhead clearance with any confidence, the same way that people hunch down when they're getting out of helicopters.

He couldn't hear me. He didn't realize that I was right behind him until it was almost too late. I had the gun in my right hand and I was shimmying up, trying to time a grab at him with my left. He was squirming along in Timberland-style boots and I was flinching back every time the ridged soles kicked only inches from my face.

I lunged and missed, but he felt me. He almost took the skin off his cheek twisting his head around on the ground to look back.

Once he'd seen me, that was it. He started to kick out wildly, thrashing his legs in a tantrum of sudden energy. Even when I managed a touch, I couldn't hold on. When I realized that he was kicking for my head I instantly ducked back, and that's when one of his boots caught my gun hand.

It wasn't a numbing blow, but it took me by surprise and sent the weapon spinning a yard or so across the concrete. That was bad. I launched myself after it, and he went after it too.

He was closer. I knew I'd be at a disadvantage if he got to it first. With him there'd be no, *Stop or I'll shoot*. It would be more a simple matter of, *Bang, you're dead.*

He got to it first.

But I was there right with him, almost hauling myself over him to clamp my hand down on top of his. He might have my gun, but as long as I had strength I was determined that he wouldn't be able to move it.

Now it was a stalemate. In a perverse way, the advantage should have been mine. He was struggling for his liberty, while I was fighting for my life. It concentrated my efforts to a remarkable degree. If I had a spare thought for anything, it was that I should have stayed on my stupid feet back there and let him go to be picked up by someone else on some other day.

He fought against my grip, I fought back against his. Our efforts canceled out and nothing moved except the truck.

Then I saw that one of its big wheels was rolling steadily toward our hands.

I turned my head and looked at him. He'd seen it, too. He met my eyes and held them as if to say, *Well*?

"You have to let go first," I said.

I could hear the tire crunching the grit that it bore down on, but I didn't take my eyes from him. He had to let go first. Had to. Any other scenario ended to my even more serious disadvantage.

He broke the staring contest to cast a quick look at the wheel. I risked a glance myself, wondering if I could take a chance on pulling my own hand away just as the rubber started to bite, leaving a couple of tons of truck to discourage my opponent's trigger finger. I'd have to move at the very last instant, right at the moment when I felt the hairs on my knuckles stir.

Which would be in about three seconds or less. Could I move that fast?

Could anyone?

He spat in my face.

I'd seen him working something around in his cheek, but I hadn't been expecting this. I flinched and shut my eyes in reflex, and knew in that moment that the struggle was lost.

He pulled his hand from under the approaching wheel, and mine came with it. Maybe if I got the other hand over and turned the gun away. But somehow it all seemed too much effort. I felt his hand slide from under mine, I felt him disengage himself from me.

He whispered something, but I don't remember what.

He took my gun and crawled away, and I just lay there as the rest of the truck slowly passed over me. The boys up in the cab had no idea of what had been taking place until they saw the man hop to his feet in front of their grille and trot away, and they knew nothing of me until they'd rolled back several yards more and saw me lying there on the ramp. By that time my own people were starting to arrive, plain clothes men on foot, uniformed officers in cruisers.

Me, I just lay there.

I heard the call go out, *Officer down.* I just wanted to say, *I'm all right, I just . . .* but it was all beyond me. I knew I wasn't hit, I knew I wasn't hurt, but I just felt so weary.

I didn't start getting scared until I tried to blink, and nothing happened.

I could hear Bob Lambert calling my name, and I could feel someone's hands on me. I heard a voice say, "I don't see him breathing," and then I was aware of someone lifting my hand from the ground and their fingertips probing around at my wrist.

Then the damnedest thing. I felt the sensation fade.

I couldn't feel the touch, I couldn't feel the ground

beneath me. I was there and aware, but it was as if I'd become separated from myself.

"There isn't any pulse," I heard the voice say.

THREE

I HEARD BOB Lambert say, "Is he hit?" and the one of the other voices reply, "Nowhere I can see," and then they turned me over onto my back and there was nothing I could do to protest or explain.

I couldn't move my eyes, either. I could see, but only what was in front of me. It was bizarre. When I tried to speak I could sense myself framing the words, but nothing happened.

No wonder they thought I was dead.

Lambert and the other sergeants were standing back and letting the uniformed men work on me. The uniforms stay more up-to-date with their emergency training. I could see my fellow-detectives in a semicircle, like an audience or a jury, but I couldn't focus my gaze on any one of them.

One of the officers started CPR. *Hey*, I wanted to say, *I don't need it*, but I could hear the breath grunting out of me as he pushed down on my chest. Worse, I could hear the creaking of my ribs as he put his full weight into it. But I felt no pain. Bob Lambert had turned his back and moved away and was using his phone.

More of our people were arriving.

I heard someone, I think it was Jimmie Noone, say, "Jesus, it's Lafcadio!" and someone else saying, "What happened to him?"

Bob Lambert was back. I heard, "Who got here first?" and then, "Was he like this when you found him?" Although the replies were beyond my hearing—I seemed to have lost the facility to filter sounds or judge direction—I could tell that the answers weren't encouraging.

I was still trying to speak. Bob Lambert took my head in both his hands and looked searchingly into my eyes. At the same time I think his fingers must have been checking for a pulse at my throat.

Come on, Bob, my mind was all but screaming at him. *I'm right here. Can't you see?*

He'd see it, surely. Even if I couldn't move for whatever reason right now, he'd have to see the spark there.

He tilted my head a little from one side to the other. It broke the eye contact and there was nothing I could do to re-establish it.

"I think you're wasting your time," he said. "He's gone."

Then he carefully lowered my head back to the ground.

They stopped working on me a while after that, and let me lie. My field of vision mostly took in everyone's shoes and the part of the ramp that was upslope from me. The bar of daylight at the top of it caused me some discomfort, but that was the only pain I felt. So even my pupils were locked and no longer responding.

They were talking about me.

"There isn't a mark on him."

"Must be something that doesn't show."

"Bruce Lee's vibrating palm of death?"

Bob Lambert said, "Come on, now. Let's get the area secured for the Crime Scene people. I'm giving Homicide a call."

The paramedics showed up right then, bringing a portable defibrillator. They set it down in front of me and I wondered what would happen if they tried to restart a heart that hadn't actually stopped yet.

But I heard Bob Lambert saying, "He's been down more than twenty minutes. Go ahead if you have to. But if you think it's a waste of time, then I'd rather not disturb the body again."

"Is that a definite twenty?"

"At least."

"Okay."

One of them opened my shirt and taped some wires, but they didn't jolt me. They took a reading in order to be a hundred per cent sure that I was beyond help, and I thought This is it, this is where they'll have to realize that I'm still here. But they ran the test and nobody made any comment at all. The machine was picked up, and they went.

Paramedics and the ambulance service only deal with the living. Once you're dead, you're someone else's department.

I wanted to scream that I was alive. I might as well have strained to levitate or turn invisible. The means to achieve it simply were not there.

Then it crossed my mind that maybe I wasn't. Alive, I mean. Maybe this was the experience of all the newly-dead. Your body dies but you don't get to leave it. God's big joke on us. The pharaohs were right.

I tried to push the thought away and concentrate on the moment, but it wouldn't quite go all the way.

My boss was filling my field of vision again. Something blurred before me and it took me a second or so to realize that he'd closed my eyes.

"What about the Crime Scene people?" Jimmy Noone said. "They get into a snit if they think you've messed with their body."

"The man's got to have some dignity," Bob Lambert said. "That wife of his made sure he had precious little of it in life."

"How so?"

"Dave Corrigan's been banging her for months. You didn't hear? He's been telling anybody who'll listen. Said how she likes it to hurt."

"Dave Corrigan from Traffic?"

"Most people knew about it. Except for Johnny-boy here. But what can you say?"

And all that, just when I'd been thinking that it couldn't possibly get any worse.

I THOUGHT I was in total darkness until someone moved across before my face and I realized that I could still see a kind of shadow play on my eyelids. It was better than nothing. That, and the sounds all around me, saved me from feeling totally adrift. I heard the homicide team arrive and break out their kits and walk through the crime scene. I'd done this myself, but I'd never even thought to imagine what it might be like from the victim's point of view. The victim wasn't supposed to *have* a point of view. I knew that I was being searched, turned over, photographed, assessed. Bags were put over my hands and taped in place. Comments were made on the absence of any visible wounds or trauma.

All that I could remember was that he'd spat in my face. Just the act. I could not, I was finding, summon up any detailed memory of what he'd looked like, what he'd said to me, or even what he'd been wearing.

Any effort I made still led to the easy sensation of movement, but with no physical counterpart. A fantasy of action, rather than action itself. I wondered if this meant that I was starting to be torn away from my body, that soon I'd break free in a burst of Industrial Light and Magic and then it would be up to the tunnel of light and grandma.

When I did move, it was because I was being lifted. I

couldn't see by whom but I assumed that it was the coroner's people with their re-usable steel shell and unmarked van. I heard the lid of the shell going on. The darkness that followed was worse than anything that had gone before.

My sense of time had already begun to slide, and I think it went completely now that I had nothing to anchor it to. I was a mind in a black box, tumbling around without even touching the walls. Some astonishing memories came up.

The next time they moved me, my eyes came slightly open again. I was in a tiled room and they were undressing me. I felt elation because I thought that I'd managed the eye-opening trick for myself, but I hadn't. I had a cross and chain that had belonged to my mother, and my lids had been moved by them working the chain off over my head.

I tried to listen to their conversation, but I couldn't follow it. They sat me up for some reason, and I saw that I was on a steel gurney with a plastic sack between my feet into which they were folding and stuffing my clothes. I didn't notice whether I'd been tagged yet.

When they'd laid me back, they wrapped me in a shroud and then they took me for a ride. I heard, "Put him right next to the door. They always fast-track it when it's a cop."

And then the next thing was cold storage and more darkness.

I'm a dead man, I thought, and I'm going to die.

My mind had cleared slightly. All of the handling must have put some fresh oxygen into my lungs or squeezed the blood around my system a little. But it wouldn't do me any good. In a matter of hours, depending on the start time of the shift and the caseload, I'd be scheduled for autopsy. I was a police officer killed on duty. The morgue attendant was right, when that happens they fast-track everything. Appalling as it was, even that thought couldn't make me break into a sweat.

I thought of them giving the news to Amy. Bitch. I'd thought I'd had no illusions about my home life, but this showed how wrong I could be. It wasn't like she was some furnace that I'd failed to keep stoked. From the time the girls were born she'd made it plain that she no longer cared much for sex at all. The slightest thing went wrong in her day, forget it. Now this? I didn't even know that she'd met Dave Corrigan, a big blond German with a buzz cut who worked in traffic patrol and looked like a henchman in a Bond movie.

If anything could rouse me from this stillness, that ought to have done it. But there I lay, amongst the dead. I knew what my feelings ought to be, but I had none of the physical effects that come with emotional states. No racing of the heart, no burning in the gut, no sinking feeling in the pit of the stomach . . .

What *had* that bastard blown in my face? And how come he could hide it in his cheek and not be affected himself? And who the hell was he?

I supposed I'd never get to know.

I was weakening, and my thoughts were losing what little coherence they had. They tumbled, like clothes in a laundromat. My best hope was that I might slip away before the true horror started. My worst fear was that it would happen and I'd continue to experience it. The most likely outcome was that they'd kill me on the slab and never even realize.

The creepiest thing I ever saw on TV was one of the old Alfred Hitchcock shows where Joseph Cotten was paralysed in an accident. They all thought he was dead, but then someone spotted a tear in his eye. Music swells, happy ending. I think they skipped over the part about him having to spend the rest of his life being turned for bedsores, fed through a tube and drained by a catheter. My mother described it to me and then years later I saw it for myself. It didn't prepare me.

Some time later, I was being moved again. I couldn't see through the shroud but I knew what was coming. I was lifted onto the table, and something was slid under my neck as the shroud was taken away.

Now I could see. My head had fallen slightly to one side. There was another autopsy already in progress on the next table. I saw the body of a young man, yellow with jaundice, his face turned toward me, his torso open from neck to crotch and his entire midsection bizarrely flayed and diminished. Our eyes were meeting like we were colleagues or companions of some kind, sharing the same grim experience.

People were moving around us. I couldn't see any faces, just their midsections in plastic aprons. The knife passed right before me in somebody's hand. They kept them sharp down here, but they didn't bother keeping them too clean. It wasn't like an operating theater. It was more like the room where they make up the animals' feed in a zoo. A place of flesh, bones, and buckets.

I heard myself being described. All my scars, the shape I was in. It was a woman's voice, not one that I knew. My friend on the next table had his face raised and turned away from me as they started in for his brain.

I did get to hear the most almighty crash as the doors came bursting open. A lot of shouting followed.

"Oh, fuck," someone said. "Tell me that's not him."

"What the hell do you think you're doing?" I heard the woman say.

"We're cops. Which one's Sergeant Lafcadio?"

"This one right here. I'm doing him now."

"Well, get the fucking knife out of him!"

"What?"

"Get the knife out of him, he isn't dead!"

The next thing that I knew was that someone was taking hold of my face and turning it so that my eyes looked into his. I saw a bearded man in a knitted wool cap, wearing a dirty loud shirt over a gray T-shirt and with his police ID on a cord around his neck. Were it not for that last detail, I might have taken him for a street hustler or a homeless person.

"It's all right, John," he said. "I know you can hear me. Everything's going to be okay."

I think they threw something over me, but for all I know they might have run me through the corridors of the building naked on a gurney, leaking from a single stigmatum just under my breastbone. I neither know nor care. The morgue was connected to the County General hospital by a second-floor walkway over the street. It had been intended for one-way traffic; I reckon I must have been the only patient in the history of the place to make the return journey.

Two of them were running with me, shouting to clear the way ahead, and I swear one of them jumped on board and rode the gurney around a couple of the corners.

I heard one say, "How deep's he cut?" and the other, the one who'd held my face and talked to me back in the autopsy suite, replied, "If he could bleed, it would kill him." And then he looked down at me and winked.

I'd have responded if I could. But I reckoned he'd understand when I didn't.

When we arrived in the emergency room, someone tried to stop us and another middle-of-the-floor argument ensued; they were elbows-deep in urgent work and it soon became obvious that there hadn't been time to call ahead, because there was resistance to the idea of dropping everything to work on a corpse at the say-so of a couple of deadbeats, until I heard somebody say, *My God, they're right, he's bleeding, look,* and I was moving again.

They shunted me into a treatment room. They shouted over me and threw modern science at me until I breathed again. I'm told it took about twenty minutes. It seemed much longer.

Apparently a single drop of fresh blood had been pumped out of the wound and had run down my chest. They later said that my heart had been beating all the way through my experience, but too slowly to be detected. My breathing was so shallow that the small amount of air in a sealed coffin would have kept me going for most of a day, which is something that I try not to dwell on.

The best feeling I've ever had was the one I had in the moment where I sat up and puked. Music swells.

But I wouldn't call myself happy, and it certainly wasn't an ending.

FOUR

A S YOU can imagine, there was a period of recuperation punctuated by one terrific bustup.

It happened early. In my hospital room, in fact. Amy had been over in Alexandria visiting her sister's family and their new baby, so they'd had trouble tracking her down. Before anyone could tell her that I was dead, I was back among the living.

Because of that, the tragedy and the miracle more or less canceled each other out. Instead of a major reappraisal of our relationship in the shadow of a life-changing event, it became a straight confrontation over her infidelity. Which apparently was all my fault. I forget why. I'd like to be able to say that our discussion was an adult one and I suppose that it was, in that much of the language was X-rated. The outcome was that by the time I was able to leave the hospital, she'd taken the girls and gone back to Alexandria and there was a realtor's sign on the lawn of my house.

I'd survived the respiratory paralysis with treatment and life-support, and in a matter of hours I'd been breathing and moving again. I could even stand the next morning, shaky as a new-born foal. It was the knife wound that extended my recovery time. There would be a medical investigation, and possibly a lawsuit. I talked to a lawyer about it, and left it in his hands. If I was due anything, fine. But I wanted to get myself back to normal, not to start a new career as a professional victim.

So the symptoms went, my family did likewise, and the cut began to heal. Only the nightmares seemed reluctant to take their leave of me, and I had some pills for those.

Bob Lambert told me to take a month off, but I went back to work after two weeks. I was given light duties, which meant a desk and a phone and an in-tray full of crap. People called by to see how I was, and I lost count of the number of times I must have told my story. I went looking for Dave Corrigan once or twice but, strange to say, he was always off on some unexplained errand.

You'd think that life would have seemed sweet after such an experience, but instead it felt somehow spoiled. I couldn't have said why, but I think I know now. We all find ways to live with the thought that we'll eventually die. I suspect that my way consisted of never quite believing that it would ever happen. My attitude was *Yeah, sure, I'll think about it someday, so don't distract me with it now.* But all that had changed. Personal mortality was no longer an abstraction that I could manage to ignore.

Not that I wasn't grateful to be alive. My rescuers didn't contact me again, and I had to ask around to find out who they were.

I was told that their names were Frank Early and Bram Shapiro, and that they were a two-man department with office space in the fifth district. Their official title was the Cult-related Crime Co-ordination Unit. I'd never heard of it before. Unofficially, they were the voodoo cops.

Every time I tried to call them, their line was busy. So the first chance I had, I ducked out of the office and drove across town to see them.

THE CHAMBER of Commerce's brochure will tell you that Iberville is a city with a small-town feel, which is about the only thing the Chamber of Commerce has managed to get right in the past twenty-five years. We have our skyscraper office blocks and our elevated freeway and the new Catholic College risen up out of the industrial wastelands on the other side of the Sabine River, but these still have the air of recent additions. They're like brand-new Nikes on a ninety-year-old.

The character of the place is solidly rooted in the nineteen-forties, all red brick and rivets, from the cantilevered iron bridge across the water to the acres of three-storied factories with their windows stoned out. I can look at the buildings on Row Street, and if I half-close my eyes I can see, not the paperback exchange or the thrift stores that stand there now, but the open newsstand with its wall of pulp magazines and the menswear outlets where my father used to buy his big pants and brown suits. The once-elegant Fairmont Hotel is still standing but it's virtually a flophouse now, with a creep at the front desk and its stately rooms subdivided into single-bedded cubicles.

I drove the elevated freeway over to the fifth district, dropping off a few blocks early to call by a place I knew that was part liquor store, part delicatessen. I wanted to pick up a couple of bottles of imported scotch whisky, the kind that come in a nice presentation box and don't just look like booze in a brown paper bag.

Fifth District Headquarters was in a '70s concrete building, a sandy-colored bunker with no street-level windows and no easy parking. I asked at the front desk for Cult Crimes, and got a blank look which vanished when I added, "Black guy and a white guy. The voodoo cops."

I found them right at the back of the building, somewhere between the locker rooms and the firing range. Their office space was barely more than a cupboard and you could hear the muffled *pop-pop-pop* of target practice through one of the walls. They waved me in and I looked for a chair, couldn't see one, and so hitched myself onto the end of a desk. Both were busy on their cell phones, while the desk phone appeared to be permanently off the hook. No wonder I'd been unable to get through.

Bram Shapiro was exactly as I remembered him. I don't think he'd even changed the shirt. I'd a less clear memory of Frank Early, beyond his color; now I saw that he was older, thinner, a tough-and-stringy type who would always seem too long-limbed for whatever chair he might have folded himself into. As I waited for one or other of them to end his call, I looked around. There were papers and magazines everywhere, a few of them in cardboard files, most just stacked up loosely. There were some spare chairs, but all had reference books heaped up on top of them and piles of National Geographics underneath. On top of a filing cabinet sat what I took to be a jokey voodoo altar, the centerpiece of which was a dirt-browned human skull with golf balls pushed into its eye sockets and a bristling all-over crown of red candles stuck on with their own melted wax. It sat in a cardboard tray lined with Spanish moss, in which nestled small toy cars.

Bram Shapiro thumbed his phone to end the call, swung his chair around to me and said, "That was Shreveport. They found a dead man in a shallow grave by a crossroads with no hands and a dozen little dolls sewn up inside him. They're wondering if there might be some ritual connection."

The next part was the embarrassing one and I got it over as quickly as I could. I thanked them for saving my life, and I gave them what I'd brought. I hadn't written a card, or anything. That would have felt stupid. They looked at the bottles and were suitably appreciative.

"This wasn't necessary," Frank Early said.

"Let the man yield to impulse," Bram Shapiro said. "Don't fence him in. How's the scar?"

"Mostly healed."

"It was a deep one."

"It's coming along fine. You want to see?"

I opened my shirt and showed them. It had stopped looking like a zipper when the stitch marks faded. Now it resembled an angry exclamation mark.

"What you actually have there is a unique conversation piece," Bram Shapiro said. "How many people can offer to show you their autopsy scar? I believe you could walk into any bar in this town and get yourself laid in twenty minutes or less, including the cab ride."

I was buttoning my shirt. "If there's ever a contest for such a thing," I said, "I'll give it a try. Anyway, show's over. And thanks again. But how did you know?"

"One of the dispatchers gave us a call," Bram Shapiro said. "She knows what we're about and she knows what to look for."

"What *are* you about?"

"Didn't they tell you?" Frank Early said. "We're the voodoo cops."

"I know about that," I said, "but I was dosed by a white guy. There was no voodoo about it."

"But you got some crap blown in your face and it nearly got you killed."

"That doesn't make it the work of the Mighty Goombah," I said. "This was for real."

"Of course it was for real," Bram Shapiro said. "Everybody thinks we mess around with the supernatural down here, but it's not *The X Files*. Most of what we deal with is crime that's specific to the Vodoun community. People's faith being used against them as a means of pressure or coercion. Like someone demanding money to lift a curse.

You can't just tell the victim to ignore it. You've got to take account of people's concerns. Let me ask you. What do you actually know about voodoo?"

"More than you probably think," I said. "I've got a spiritualist church at the end of my street. Half my neighbors are in the congregation. It looks just like any other religion to me."

"Well, that's right," Bram Shapiro said. "Every religion addresses the same human need. Each one tries to mirror the vast unknowable universe in the shape of a story. The next thing you know is, we're at war because my story's factual and yours is just superstition. Vodoun's the African story, mainly out of the tribes around the Gulf of Benin. It got exported with the slaves and refined for the New World, and then the movies screwed around with it and turned it into horror show stuff full of human sacrifice and the walking dead."

"And women dancing naked," Frank Early said. "You always miss out the best part."

"They've got Catholic saints," I said.

"Yeah, they'll take in anything. As religions go, Vodoun's more flexible than most. It recognizes that there's all kinds of ways to tell the story."

"And this ties in with some white boy spitting nerve poison in my eyes . . . how, exactly?"

Frank Early said, "This is no ordinary white boy. He's a special kind of parasite and we'd been warned he might be coming our way."

"What you got in the face was a cocktail of natural poisons known more to folk-magic than to science," Bram Shapiro said. "Magic is the idiot cousin of religion. At least religion's making an attempt to pick some kind of meaning out of the big mystery. Practising magic to get what you want is like laughing at the TV to make Frasier come on. Anyone who plans to make a living from it needs a few secret tricks to deliver the occasional result."

I looked from one to the other. "So you're saying he's--- what? Like a white rapper? The Marshall Mathers of voodoo?"

Shapiro made a search-me face. "Simple answer? We don't know who he is. We've had about five different versions of the story and they all start in Louisiana State Prison. Some say he shared a cell with a so-called vodoun priest awaiting trial for statutory rape. One version is that he asked to be initiated, and the rules of vodoun say he couldn't be turned down. Another says that he made the necessary calls to make his teacher's troubles go away so the rape trial couldn't happen."

Frank Early added, "We went through five years of prison records but we couldn't verify any of it. Which means nothing either way."

"This teacher was supposed to be what they call a bocu, an outsider who sells his skills to do harm. It's very hard to distinguish the realities from the bullshit in all of this. In one version his pupil's called George Boyd, in another he's Jean Deroche. Neither's a known name or an alias."

"We do know that he tried calling himself Legendre for a while, but nobody would take him seriously."

"Two years ago he turns up in California offering his services as a Vodoun spiritual advisor. He was using more than one name and targeting lifestyle faddists."

"You know the kind of people?" Frank Early said. "Shave your head and you're a Buddhist. I dumped my astrologer for a personal shaman. Feng Shui is *so* last year."

Bram Shapiro said, "He was like a walking stupidity tax. All he needed was to place ads in the style magazines and wait for the phone to ring. They let him into their lives and he cleaned them out. Within a year he'd put quite a fortune together, but then one of his victims unexpectedly grew a brain. The San Rafael cops didn't find him, but they got to his money before he did and froze it. He wasn't quite as sharp a financier as he was a con man. He fled the state and we think he came home to start over. This time he took more care over how he controlled his people."

I said, "Like kidnapping their children?"

"Keeping them in fear of something like it, at least," Frank Early said.

Shapiro added, "The woman from the mall is obviously one of his . . . I don't know what you'd call them. Clients? It doesn't matter how he screws them over, they're always too scared to fight back. The minute she knew her boy was safe, the woman started having problems with her memory."

They weren't surprised that I'd no memory of my own regarding what he looked like. Some of his poisons acted like a chemical reset button for the victim's short-term recall, they said. I found it strange that I seemed to have forgotten his face and nothing else.

Maybe that was what he'd told me to do, when he'd whispered those words that I couldn't remember.

I left after a while, before we ran out of things to talk about and it started getting awkward. It wasn't worth my going back to the office, so I called to check for messages (none) and then I headed for home.

FIVE

THE REALTY company sign was staked into the scrubby strip of lawn that passed for my front yard. I parked the Jeep on the driveway alongside it and walked to the front door, digging out my keys as I went. The Boxleitners' blind retriever was barking as usual so as usual I called across the street, "It's me," and it shut up.

I liked my house. I liked where it was. Ours was a frankly oddball neighborhood and although I've seen others exactly like it in many other towns, I still have no idea of how they come to be. Each house stands on its own lot and almost no two are quite the same. The families of skilled bluecollar workers live right alongside newlywed low-paid professionals. Black and white get along side by side. Most of the houses are one-story frame buildings but you can get a near-mansion sited right next to a trailer home with a plywood skirt. People live out in their yards a lot, and keep old furniture there for the purpose.

I'll resist the temptation to score points off Amy but I have to tell you, she was never comfortable here and she was always looking forward to the day we'd move out. I'd see some of the places she had her eye on, and I'd have to think of non-confrontational ways of grounding her ambitions for a while. Those new gated communities out by the lake were simply beyond our means, and although the pretty wedding-cake houses in Iberville's garden district were surprisingly affordable, that was because they combined the disadvantages of a money pit with those of a crime target.

What did that leave? Places little different to the one we were already in.

I hooked the front door shut behind me and walked through the house to the bedroom, shrugging out of my suit coat as I went. I still had to get used to the feel of returning to an empty home. Amy couldn't keep the girls in Alexandria for ever—they had school to return to in three weeks' time—but she planned to find an apartment to be paid for with her share of the money from the sale, and I was to find something similar.

My heart sank at the prospect of moving. They say that moving house is a trauma on a par with the death of a close relative. To which I say, if you're giving me a choice, fetch me the gun.

I changed into chinos and a T-shirt, and added my laundry to the growing heap on the floor. I started to walk away from it, but then sensed that the five days' worth had reached the necessary critical mass to generate male guilt and so I went back and gathered it all up in my arms.

Our washing machine was in the garage. Like everybody else's, our garage was full of junk we'd half-thrown out while our cars, the most expensive items we owned, lived out on the street. The interior of the garage was dark, but it wasn't cool; it was like the entire day's humidity had built up in there, and I broke into a sweat as soon as I stepped inside. As I was loading the machine, a big cockroach scuttled out from underneath it. Quick as a flash, I stamped on it and heard it crack. And then remembered I was barefoot.

I was wiping the sole of my foot on the grass in the backyard when I heard a voice calling out to me, "Hey, Mister Lafcadio."

I looked over my shoulder and saw a black teenaged boy hanging over my gate. When I say a teenager, I'm talking about eighteen or nineteen. It was Michael Zeno, the Reverend Zeno's youngest boy.

I said, "Hi there, Michael."

"Did you eat yet?"

"Just about to."

"Missus Dodds said to tell you when I saw you. They're having a cook-out this evening."

"Is this a regular barbecue, or does Johnny Dodds have another idea to try out on us?"

"You guessed it," Michael said. "Warn your stomach, it's another journey into the unknown."

"What is it this time?"

"I'm sworn not to tell. He's proud of this one. Starts in half an hour."

"Tell them I'll be there."

Well, that solved the problem of choosing what to eat tonight. Another aspect of the carefree single life that I was having to adapt to. I went inside and checked the beer stock in the refrigerator, just to be sure that I had enough to take along.

Johnny Dodds was a barbecue junkie for whom char-broiling was no longer enough of a challenge or a satisfaction. His last innovation had been the Blowtorch Steak. I'd been there when he'd steamed catfish in an old dishwasher. I'd tried filet mignon cooked on the engine block of his car. Most of his ideas had worked out in one way or another, although the neighborhood had drawn the line at his Chicken Sushi. At his cookouts, he hung suitcase-sized speakers from his windows and played Grateful Dead music. In theory there was no-one to be disturbed by the noise, because everyone within earshot got an invitation. In practice I usually left early, before the inevitable arrival of one of our patrols to break it up.

When the crockery in my kitchen started to jump to

the bass, I locked up the house and headed down the street with a case of beer under my arm. Turning the corner, I could see that a few people had already arrived and that some had brought their own chairs. Five little girls were crammed into the seat on the teak garden swing that I'd built for the Dodds in exchange for babysitting, a good eight or nine years before. Their ten legs kicked like a caterpillar's as they swung, and I hoped that the frame was still good. I'd been a carpenter before I'd become a police officer. My one point of resemblance to Harrison Ford, until I got a sexy scar of my own and made it two.

The evening's experiment was already under way. At a safe distance from the house—a move which placed the danger rather closer to my own, if you considered the way that the lots backed onto one another—a metal tank had been welded onto the framework of a tubular steel table. There was a chain hoist directly above the tank, supported on a pole between a couple of stepladders. Johnny Dodds and a couple of others were watching critically as Michael Zeno fiddled with the jets of a propane burner underneath, trying to get the flames just right.

I went to put my beers into the common ice bucket. This was near to where Johnny Dodds' brother was standing, sucking his teeth and watching his sibling's labors with an expression of doubt.

I said, "What was the tank used for before this?" and Johnny's brother shook his head slowly.

"The first person who said that was sorry he asked," he said.

"Did it at least get scrubbed out?"

He held out his hands. They were raw-looking, and the knuckles were skinned.

"With a pressure hose and steel wire brushes," he said.

"Took three of us the entire afternoon."

The sky darkened ominously as more people arrived, but the weather seemed to hold. Lightbulbs slung in the branches of the trees were switched on. Someone had brought along their own CDs and put on something lower-key and more bearable. Johnny was too preoccupied to notice.

The tank had been three-quarters filled with cooking oil. As the propane jets got this up to temperature, Johnny went into the house and came out with an entire plucked and dressed turkey. Anything bigger would have been an ostrich. Its claw feet were still on and had been wired together at the ankles.

Johnny and Michael attempted to attach this to the chain hoist by ascending the supporting ladders with the bird between them. They hadn't thought this part through too well, but they got the turkey onto the hook after a certain amount of Laurel-and-Hardying.

I saw an empty chair over on the lawn next to the Reverend Henry, Michael Zeno's father, and I went and sat beside him. The Reverend was watching his son's efforts with an expression that hovered somewhere between doubt and pain.

Without taking his eyes off the scene, he said, "How's your health, now, John?"

"I'm all mended, Henry," I told him.

"Body and soul?"

"Soul still needs a little work."

Johnny Dodds worked the hoist, hauling on the chain, and the turkey descended into the heated tank like a trussed-up hero into a torture device. Only there was no escape for this sorry bird. It's hard for me to describe the noise that it made when it dunked into the oil. It was both searing and roaring, like a red-hot sword being plunged into water while a rocket blasted off in the background. I'd swear that everybody breathed in at the same moment and the lights seemed to dim for a second.

The Reverend Zeno said, "You any closer to catching the feller?"

"Not my job to do it," I said. "They've got me answering the phone and taking it easy. It's like I'm halfway retired already."

"Seems strange not to set you on him. You having the motivation, and all."

"Well, that's the way they work it. It's not supposed to be personal. They've got the voodoo cops on this one."

He looked at me then. I could never put an age on the Reverend. Michael was the youngest of his seven children, and he was around nineteen. But I knew of another son who lived away and worked for the Hibernia National Bank, and he was at least my age.

He said, "The voodoo cops? Bram Shapiro still doing that job?"

"Him and Frank Early. Know them?"

"Met them once or twice. In the course of mutual business."

I told him what they'd told me. About the self-styled bocu who'd learned the tricks and the patter and had been preying on the gullible middle classes, and how almost none of his victims would speak out against him. While we were talking, the turkey was hauled out, stabbed with a meat thermometer, and plunged back in.

The Reverend said, "Sounds like he's formed himself a secret society of one. Kind of a one-man white bizango."

"A what?"

"A bizango. It's a secret society of black magicians. Don't you watch any movies? They're the ones who are supposed to make the zombies."

"I don't think he's any kind of a believer. It's pretty obvious he's just lifted some of the drill for his own devices."

"Belief isn't everything. Not believing in gravity doesn't mean you won't stick to the ground. The drill mostly comes down to one thing, and that's poison of one kind or another. I grew up across the river. I've seen people die, I've seen them waste away, I've seen them down on their knees and barking like a dog. You could go to a scary guy and he'd fix it to happen for you. They wanted you to believe they had a special power, but you think about it. Everybody's got to drink, everybody's got to eat, everybody's got to breathe."

"That's what they reckoned. But they still don't know exactly what I got dosed with. Where do you pick up that kind of knowledge?"

"It's around, it's underground. They call it Petro. It's angry slave magic. Believe me. That's a world you do not want to enter."

"I think I'm already in it."

"No," he said. "You just got a closer look into it than most. Leave the rest to the voodoo cops. They know what to watch out for."

Big as it was, the entire turkey was cooked in about twenty minutes. Sliced and served with corn fritters bulk-fried in a hanging plant basket, it was like something from the menu that killed Elvis. For once, I didn't have to leave before the end of the party; the party ended prematurely.

That sky hadn't just been darkening, it had been ripening, and the downpour started with no more warning than a single lightning flash and then a bang like a starting-pistol. Johnny ran to cover the tank, and everyone else picked up their chairs and ran for home. When it rains around here, it rains all at once. It's over soon enough, but it leaves you in too sorry a state to go on enjoying yourself.

And I had been, kind of. Enjoying myself, I mean. I'd felt as if I'd been going through the motions over these past few weeks, bobbing for apples in the diaper bucket of life. My marriage was a train wreck, my house was on the market, and my boss was too embarrassed to look me in the eye. Something had to change.

I stepped between a couple of nine-year-olds who'd taken shelter under the overhang of my house, sitting and watching the raindrops bouncing on their bicycles where they'd abandoned them on the concrete sidewalk. A blue mist was rising from the ground everywhere the rain hit.

"You okay there?" I said, and they said that they were. With Amy or the girls in the house I'd have invited them to wait inside, but being here on my own I knew better than to risk that Boo Radley factor. They'd be gone as soon as the rain ended, and the rain would end in a minute or less.

Such was my sense of well-being that I tried sleeping that night without my prescription pills. They were nothing magical, just a powerful sedative that were meant to make me sleep so deeply that I either wouldn't dream, or would wake with no recollection of the dreams that I'd had. The downside involved feeling slurry and blurry for the first few hours of every day, and I'd begun to fantasize twitches and tremors on the slightest evidence. I wasn't supposed to take them with alcohol. So . . .

It wasn't the greatest idea. The nightmare I had was as assured and hideous as ever, and it was probably made far worse by the bellyful of deep-fried turkey that pinned the center of me to the bed like a mud anchor. Once more I was immobilized, and my faceless assailant was looking deep into my eyes and telling me, *You're mine now, even your soul is mine.*

I woke at around four in the morning, and went into the bathroom. I propped myself one-handed against the wall and, during an endless beer pee, tried as hard as I could to construct some mental image of the man who'd damaged me. But I couldn't. In spite of the fact that we'd looked into each other's eyes and our faces had been only inches apart, I'd no sense or picture of his.

Which meant that I could meet him again, and I wouldn't even know it.

Now, *that* was scary.

I went back to bed and tried to sleep, but the next hour or so passed in dozes and fitful spells of wakefulness. In the end I got up with the dawn, and sat in the kitchen with coffee and those strange shows that precede early-morning TV. With pills, without them, it seemed I just couldn't win.

Something had to change, all right.

SIX

MY FIRST sight of Julie Boudreaux's property was of a high wire fence with an electric gate and no direct line of sight to the house beyond it. Just waxy-looking bushes and cypress trees crowded up on the other side of the mesh. A remote-controlled camera looked down on me from a high pole within the compound, while right by the gate there was a box with a red button and a speaker-phone. The camera had lights mounted to either side of it, photoflood bulbs like big fly eyes.

I got out of my vehicle and as I was walking toward the gate, two good-sized guard dogs came down the driveway at a run and hit the wire from the other side. They hung onto the links with their claws so that they could stand up at full height while doing their best to deafen me. I recognized them as a couple of Catahoula curs, bred to herd wild cattle and hogs but also good for hunting and security work.

They appeared to have the run of the grounds. I pressed the red button and when their barking got even louder, I wondered how I was going to make myself heard or hear anything back from the speaker.

But the problem had obviously arisen before, because the box volume was turned up high. When it crackled into life, I heard a terse, "*What?*"

I held my ID up at arm's length for the camera to see. "John Lafcadio, ma'am," I said.

"*You can see the dogs. Please go away.*"

"That's Sergeant Lafcadio, ma'am, we met at the mall when your son was missing." The camera didn't move, and I put my ID back into my coat.

"*I've got nothing more to say to the police. Call my lawyer.*"

"Which do I tell him about? Your short memory or your base ingratitude?"

"*Excuse me?*"

"I nearly died for you and your kid. I'm still not right from it."

"*Nobody asked you to.*"

Well, that was hard to argue with. I searched for a riposte, but I couldn't muster one.

"Unbelievable," I muttered, making sure I muttered it loudly enough for the box to pick it up. Shaking my head, I turned to go. But not too fast.

"*Wait,*" she said.

I stopped. After a few moments, the two dogs abruptly ceased their barking and dropped to the ground before heading off in the direction from which they'd appeared. If there had been a signal of any kind, I hadn't heard it.

Shortly after that, there was a buzz and the gate started to roll open.

I drove through, and checked my mirror to see the gate closing again behind me. There was woodland for about a hundred yards or more and then it cleared and I could see the house.

It was modern, white, architect-designed. It made me think of a space-aged version of those Kenyan safari lodges on stilts. The garages and utilities were underneath and the living space started one story up, with an open deck all around it. From here it looked all slabs and angles, like a badly-stacked club sandwich.

She was standing at the deck rail, waiting for me.

The closer I got, the less like money it looked. The stucco was grubby and there were streaks under the windows. The land on which it stood had been cleared for some distance all around, but it hadn't been cultivated. The effect was like that of a once-expensive house going to seed in the middle of a bomb crater.

"Use the stairs," she called down to me.

I was a little wary as I got out of the car, but the Catahoula dogs didn't reappear. I've heard that people hunt bears with them. I felt safer when I'd reached the deck.

She hadn't waited, but had gone into the house ahead of me. The entrance was around the other side, I imagine to preserve the lines and the look. As I went around, the deck passed right over the dogs' enclosure. I glanced down and saw them circling in their limited space like a couple of turds in a whirlpool.

It was a long room, low-ceilinged, white walls. At its far end, a broad spiral staircase led up to the next level. There was a castiron hood for a log fire which wasn't lit. The floor was terracotta tile without a rug in sight, and I thought I could see a few marks on the plaster where art might once have hung. I couldn't work out if the effect was a product of minimalism or locusts.

Julie Boudreaux was wearing a soft knitwear top in rust brown, and some tan stretch pants. Neither was anything special but both looked expensive.

She was well-groomed, well-kept, high-maintenance. All this on a frame that gave her a genetic head-start on the rest of the field. But it was don't-touch perfection. The best description I've heard of her type is that they dress well not to attract men, but to annoy other women.

Standing well back from me, she said, "What do you want, Mister Lafcadio?"

"Coffee would be nice," I said, only half-seriously.

"It might, if you were staying."

"Tell me what's wrong," I said. "I can understand how you'd be frightened to speak to just anyone. But why won't you talk to me?"

"I don't choose to."

"He's got you that scared?"

"Believe what you like."

"I don't get this," I said. "People put their lives at risk to help you, me included. Why are you determined to be such hard work?"

"What are you going to tell me?" she said. "That you can protect us? You're wasting your time, detective. You can't."

"How did you meet him?"

She said nothing.

"What name did he give you?"

She didn't even avoid meeting my eyes. Kept up that even stare, daring me to go on. *Keep talking, don't expect any co-operation, I'm fascinated to see how long it will take you to get the message.*

I said, "I can't tell you how much it would help us if we could get hold of his real name. Not Legendre, or Jean Deroche, or the Great Bam-Boo or whatever he was calling himself when you invited him into your lives."

She glanced away and I thought she was going to say something then, but I was wrong. Instead of answering me, she went over to the spiral stairway and raised her voice to call up it.

"Christopher?" she said. "Come down here."

Then she turned to look at me again.

"I'm guessing now," I persisted. "Tell me if any of this is close. He started by taking a look around the place and then telling you that you were right to call him. Your lives were . . . I don't know, out of balance, something to do with the spirits, someone was wishing you harm or making you suffer and you needed him to turn the evil forces away. So then what? He gave you new names, voodoo names? Rituals that you had to follow? He'd have you work over your interior decor, definitely. What was it like in here before you stripped it all out? Let me guess."

I started to move in a circle around the room toward her, looking at the marks on the floor where stuff had been, trying to build up a picture. The fact was that the room gave me no clues at all. I was winging it, completely.

"Haitian colors and ethnic furniture," I said. "Driftwood, bones, chicken feet and candles . . . really made you feel like you were living the life. Where was your voodoo altar?"

She was still giving me the mute stare. But I knew that I must be getting to her a little because the stare was growing harder, brighter. I hadn't seen anything like it since a pissed-off Mike Nesmith stonewalling his way through interviews on the Monkees reunion tour.

And still I persisted. "Then something happened," I said, stopping in front of her. "Something good. A piece of luck or an unexpected development. Something that couldn't be explained any other way than by saying, Hey, he knows his stuff. This is actually working."

I was thinking about Bram Shapiro's laughing-at-the-TV analogy. Do it for a whole week and you'd eventually get your proof. I became aware of the boy descending the stairway to join us.

"What then?" I said. "Once he's got you believing, his manner turns all grave . . . the spiritual threat runs deeper than he'd ever imagined. It's not enough to turn your home into the McVoodoo house. He needs to clean up your business affairs, purify your finances in accordance with the principles of whatever. How am I doing?"

The boy was standing beside his mother now. He

looked stiff-limbed and awkward, like he'd been scrubbed and dressed for church on Sunday and then rolled out for inspection.

Julie Boudreaux said, "This is Sergeant Lafcadio. He saved you from that strange man who tried to take you. Thank him."

He looked at me.

"Thank you, sir," he said.

I said, "But he wasn't a stranger to you, was he, Christopher?"

But Christopher said nothing. He just stared at me, too.

Then he cast a shifty little glance at his mother and she quickly said, "You can go back up now."

So he turned right around and back up he went, still walking as if there was a key in his back.

I watched him all the way until his feet disappeared from sight. No further sound came from above.

"And that's it," I said.

"We're out of coffee. Sorry."

"You didn't tell me how close I got with my version of events."

She leaned toward me, as if she was about to impart a secret, and she lowered her voice so that her son wouldn't be able to hear.

"You think we're that fucking shallow?" she said. "Goodbye, detective."

"Your boy's not in school."

"He's been unwell."

"Same thing as your husband?"

"That is *so* cheap."

I offered her a card.

"That's a direct number on the back," I said.

She wouldn't take it. Left me holding it out for as long

as I could stand looking stupid. After a few moments I laid it down on the nearest surface, a plain hardwood table just like the ones in the store at the mall.

I said, "Do I get a head start on the Hounds of Zaroff?"

"Just be on the right side of the gate when it closes," she said.

She was hard work, all right. She didn't follow me out to my car. I looked up in case she'd come to the rail for some parting word, but she hadn't. I saw the boy's pale face at the window above, though, and when he saw me looking at him he dodged back and out of sight.

The gate was open when I got to the end of the driveway, and it was already starting to close again before I'd made it halfway through.

SEVEN

LATER IN the week I had to take myself along to an office in a plaza in the middle of town for yet another medical check. This one wasn't part of my treatment, but had been ordered by the department to ensure that I was fit to continue with the tasks they'd assigned me. It was work that wouldn't have challenged the feeblest man in town, but I had to be looked at anyway. Doctor Gaynor took my pressure, listened to my lungs, looked at my chest and said, "You know what that scar looks like?"

"You can stop right there," I said quickly.

"You never saw *Videodrome*?"

"Don't know it," I said. "How much longer before I can get off this 'light duties' caper?"

He indicated for me to put my shirt back on. "That's your boss's decision," he said. "Not mine."

"So in your opinion I'm fit?"

"What do you want me to tell you? You're no worse than most."

"Thanks," I said. "You know anything about the St Francis Center?"

"Why? Thinking of checking yourself in?"

"Interested in someone who did." I didn't see much point in telling him that the someone in question was a certain Mr Kenneth (Kenny) Boudreaux. The name would have meant nothing to him.

"It's a facility for long-term psychiatric care. Mostly self-referrals. You can sit around in your skivvies, get lots of drugs and daytime TV. Not one of the best."

"How so?"

"It's up to minimum clinical standard," Doctor Gaynor said, "but it's what you'd have to call a no-frills operation. In this life, you mostly get what you pay for."

The drive back through town took me along Row Street. I could never pass through this area without thinking how the city could really do something with it, how the buildings might be crumbling but if you took away the plastic signs and opened the boarded-up sections, their basic character was intact. The girls would make fun of me because I always said the same thing and they could always guess it was coming. But nothing ever improved around here, and it was always true.

My eye was caught by a red Mazda in one of the meter bays on the parking side of the street. Not so much by the car but by the six unrepaired bullet holes that punctured its hood.

I turned around by the Fairmont and came back down the other side of the street, passing closer to reassure myself that I hadn't been mistaken. I hadn't. There was plenty of space further down, so I turned around once more and pulled in.

Most of the buildings here stood completely empty and it was only the street-level storefronts that were still in use. It wasn't quite as low as a porno district, but it was moving that way. Right now it was what you might call low-rent lively. Tattoo and piercing parlors, vinyl record stores, a couple of basement jazz clubs. Down one of the side-streets there was a walk-in day center for drug abusers.

About fifty yards down from the red Mazda stood a Voodoo Gift Shop.

Yes, we had one of those. It incorporated a voodoo museum in a couple of back rooms and as far as I knew, it was exclusively aimed at tourists. I'd certainly never heard of any trouble involving the place. Going by their window they sold stuff like handmade African crafts, voodoo kits, oils, candles, and posters. Thursdays and Saturdays they advertised a psychic in attendance, no appointments necessary.

But there was the red Mazda, standing almost right outside the door. That couldn't be coincidence. Could it?

My heart was rattling too fast, and my chest felt unnaturally tight. I watched the store for a while longer but nobody came out or went in, and I finally had to ask myself if I was planning to sit here forever with a shut-tight puckered-up behind, or if I was going to make a move.

Of course, I could always just call it in.

Alternatively, I could forget I'd ever seen anything, and drive away.

But I checked my new gun and I got out of the car.

I call it new, but it was the burglar gun that I'd previously kept in the bedroom and loaded with blanks. While you don't want to be loosing off live rounds in a thin-walled house with your family all around you, nor do you want to feel completely undefended. Even a starting-pistol would do it. Blast off at your average intruder in a confined space and darkness, and you'll be left with nothing but a blur toward the window and a streak of liquid shit left hanging in the air.

Since losing my real gun to the so-called bocu, I'd promoted the burglar gun and I'd taken to keeping it on me most of the time. Nobody was ever going to spit in my eye again. I didn't plan to let anyone get that close.

I didn't walk to the Voodoo Shop but instead went around the back of the block and counted down the doorways in the alley. It was easy enough to locate the one I needed. The comics shop next door had thrown out a stack of cardboard point-of-sale material, and fanboys rummaging for goodies had cut the strings on the bales so that their contents were spilled all around.

Someone had forced a window, up on the second floor. The room inside stank of human waste and there was evidence of what had to have been the grimmest party ever known to man. There were some rags and a mattress that I wouldn't have touched with a pair of tongs. I went through the room and into a stairway where the plaster had been ripped from the walls exposing the wooden laths beneath. While descending I put my weight on the outsides of the risers, in case they decided to creak.

Down at the bottom there was a panel door that had been all but destroyed. It led into a narrow passageway with a locked gate at one end and the rear door of the Voodoo Shop at the other. This door showed evidence of past attempts to force entry, including setting a trash fire at the base of it, but it looked as if it had withstood them all.

Someone had been out here, slashing empty Lucky Gator cartons and stamping them flat. The door to the gift shop was unbolted.

I flowed in there like oil. Well, in my mind I did. An observer would have seen a middle-aged man sliding along the wall with not much grace but intense concentration. At a doorway I paused and checked out an empty room with a kitchen counter and some rudimentary coffee making equipment . . . an electric kettle, milk in a carton, mugs that had been rinsed too many times and washed too few. The next room contained a card table and a threadbare tarot pack and a table lamp with a red tasseled shade, unlit.

The passageway ended in a right-angled turn and a bead curtain. Out in the shop, I could hear voices. Two men talking. I looked through the beads and saw a white male leaning on the counter on the customer side, a black male behind it.

At that point I lowered the gun and stepped through the curtain.

The black guy spun around at the rattling sound. "Hey!" he protested.

On the other side of the counter, Bram Shapiro said, "Relax, Freddie, he's a cop."

But Freddie was less than impressed, and clearly displeased by the intrusion. "So he can't use the front door like everyone else?" he demanded.

"Forgive me," I said. "I saw a car out front that gave me reason to be nervous."

Shapiro glanced through the window. "That one?" He had to dodge his head around a little to get a line of sight on the car in the street outside. "That's mine," he said. "We requisitioned it."

I was putting the gun away and moving around to the public side of the counter. "I'm surprised that it's fit to go back on the road," I said. "I must have shot it six times."

"Yeah, and missed everything there was to hit. With you on the case, Bonnie and Clyde could have made it to a sequel. Freddie Small, meet John Lafcadio. He's the one I called you about."

Freddie inspected me. He was about thirty, thin-lipped, light-skinned, well-spoken, still a touch pissed-off.

"The coma cop?" he said.

"The very one."

"In that case I suppose I should make allowances," he said. But even then I can't say that he seemed too forgiving.

I looked around. There were masks on the wall, along with display cards of amulets and talismans. Other counter displays carried potions, herbs, roots, incense . . . there were fake human skulls, and more candles than St Patrick's at Easter.

"No need to ask what you do for a living," I said.

"Don't jump to conclusions," Shapiro said. "Freddie's no ordinary storekeeper. He's got a diploma. What was it in, Freddie? Neurobiology?"

"Neurochemistry," Freddie said.

I looked down at one of the boxed voodoo kits under the counter glass and said, "So what's the chemical basis for 'other-side's-lawyer-be-stupid'?"

"Sometimes the power's all in the label."

"Got anything that's good for bad dreams?"

"Bad dreams are just a sign to your real trouble. You need to work out who's burning a candle against you."

Bram Shapiro said, "Did you go up there yet? How'd you get along with the mother?"

"Finish your business," I told him. "I'll wait."

I moved away and scanned some of the other stuff in the shop as I half-listened to their conversation, which was mostly gossip about people I'd never heard of. Shapiro might have seemed to be killing time, but I could see that he was doing rather more than that. He was networking, checking on certain people, putting in some time to maintain one of his avenues of information.

From the way they were talking, it sounded as if Freddie Small was probably a well-connected figure in the Vodoun community. There was probably some kind of a business behind the business, because on the face of it his shop was mostly stocked with what I'd have called novelties. As well as voodoo kits for all occasions (Luck Around Business, Boss-Fix Powder, Come to Me Drops) he'd a rack of books, voodoo music tapes, voodoo calendars, readymade gris-gris bags for various ailments and purposes . . . even T-shirts and bumper stickers.

"I told her, passing a black stool ain't a sign of wickedness," Freddie Small was saying. "You tell him he's got to see his doctor."

When they'd done, I walked out with Shapiro. Once we were on the sidewalk I started to tell him about my visit to Julie Boudreaux.

"From the look of the place I'd say they've been taken for everything they had," I said, "and he's still looking for more."

"You did better than me," Shapiro said. "I never even got past those dogs and the spy camera."

"What do you know about the husband?"

"Kenny Boudreaux? Got rich with a land development company. Took helicopter lessons and drove a Mercedes. Big man, big noise, folded like origami when it all turned against him. He checked himself into the hospital and left his wife to deal with the incoming fire. Give me one like her any day. She ain't helpful, but she's tough. Did you eat yet?"

"Not yet."

"Why don't you follow me?"

I was about to say that I had to get home. But it wasn't true. I didn't. That was a reflex, born of years of habit. Nobody waited there for me now.

So I said, "Yeah. Why don't I."

I DROVE behind him and he led me to a new-looking, square building out on the Memorial Parkway where all the big car dealerships are. No frills here, just a neon Budweiser sign and the name *Mama's*. It had no windows and there were about a dozen vehicles outside. It could equally have been a place you'd go to for elegant cocktails or butt-ugly lapdancers.

Inside, it had dark brick walls and an open kitchen. Its menu was a list of beers, with the food listed separately on a board above the bar. Although it wasn't yet six, the place was already beginning to fill up with a mixture of manual workers and office types. We sat at a round table. The waitress who took our order seemed to know Shapiro well.

When she'd left us I said, "So what's the story with the Mazda?"

"I should have explained," Shapiro said. "While you were down, your man escaped on foot and left his car behind. We traced ownership to a woman in the garden district. Long dress and bangles and a house full of cats. Seems he'd been living in a cottage on her property. She'd been feeding him, buying him stuff, introducing him to new contacts. She wouldn't give us anything more than she had to, but in her case I reckon it's more through loyalty than fear. From where she sees it, we're persecuting a genius. She insisted that the car was a no-strings gift. So once we'd processed it, we kept it for the job."

"Think she's got a way to reach him?"

"Who knows? If I had the manpower I could put surveillance on her. As it is, there's just me and Frank and life's too short."

Something came up on the jukebox, and everybody at that end of the room booed. I looked over my shoulder, surprised to see how much the place had filled up in such a short time.

Frank Early joined us around then. Bram Shapiro shouted something into his ear over the rising noise.

"You actually got to talk to the Boudreaux woman?" Frank Early said.

"Yeah, but don't be impressed," I said. "It was short and none too fruitful."

"That's not necessarily a bad thing," Early said. "As long as he knows she's too scared to give him up, there's a good chance that our spook will come back to the well. In the meantime, you got a foot in the door."

We had to hitch our chairs in to make room for the parties of office workers that were squeezing onto the tables around us now. Most of them were thirty or under, affluent and unpartnered, although I don't believe it was a singles bar as such. They were here because work was over and they'd no pressure to get themselves home.

Encouraged by my success in talking to Julie Boudreaux, even though I seemed to have achieved nothing by it, Frank Early gave me a more detailed rundown of our nameless spook's known history. I was aware of Bram Shapiro tuning out and taking more of an interest in the party of eight on the table right behind us, all women.

Frank Early said, "When he was operating in California he made himself more than three million in a couple of years, but because he'd left a paper trail they were able to seize and freeze every penny of it. Since he came home he's been operating strictly in cash." He leaned closer. "Guess where he was keeping his money."

I waited.

"We found it in the car," Frank Early said. "In the well under the spare. What a loser."

"So he's broke again?"

"Unless he keeps an emergency wad stowed up his ass, I'd imagine so."

"If he came here from California, what's the FBI position?"

"They've opened a file," Frank said, and the face he made suggested that they'd done exactly that, and nothing more.

Mama's was one of those bars where they don't give you a glass unless you ask for one. I was taking a pull from the bottle when Bram Shapiro gave me a shove on the shoulder that almost made me knock my front teeth loose.

"Wounded in the line of duty?" I heard him saying. "This is the man you ought to be talking to."

I looked around and gave what I hoped was a pleasant smile, and then I turned back and dabbed at my lips with a napkin just to check that my gums weren't bleeding.

The food came and the evening wore on. The place was heaving by now and it felt like it was around ten o'clock, but when I checked my watch I saw that it wasn't yet eight.

I said to Frank, "Where are the rest rooms?" and he pointed.

When I got back, my place had been taken by one of the women from the next table who was working hard on Frank Early, leaning close to him, touching his arm, telling him what appeared to be her entire life story. One of her co-workers saw me hesitating, and beckoned me to the empty seat beside her.

"Your friend's been telling me all about you," she said.

"I bet," I said.

"They were actually on the point of cutting you open?"

"Yeah, they even made a start."

"He said if I was nice to you, I might get to see the scar."

"It's not something I tend to show off in public."

"Who said anything about in public?"

Well, what can I tell you? The next thing I know is, she's leaning close to me, touching my arm, telling me her whole life story. She'd hated her first job and had retrained as a book-keeper, although given a choice she'd be a full-time henna tattooist. But there wasn't a living to be made from that. About an hour and four beers later, a cab picked us up and took us to her apartment in a converted sugar warehouse. There was no elevator and she gripped my hand tightly as she led me up to her floor. I felt as if I was falling with every step.

Once inside, within a second or two of the door closing, she was saying, "So. Do I get to see it, or not?"

"Seriously?"

"Unless you came here under false pretences."

I reached to unbutton my shirt, but she stopped me. She wanted to do it herself.

"Wow," she said. "How deep does it go?"

"I couldn't tell you."

"Will it hurt if I touch it?"

"It's just a mark."

Quite unexpectedly, she leaned forward and tilted her head to one side and ran the tip of her tongue along the length of the scar.

And I swear to you, by the time she reached the end of it, every last hair on my body was standing erect.

IT WAS sometime after midnight when I woke up beside her and remembered where I was. I'd no reason to feel guilty, but I could tell that the habit was going to die hard. My head was a lot clearer than it had been. I eased out of her bed and picked my clothes up off the floor.

When I was dressed, I leaned over her and said, "I have to go."

She murmured into her pillow, something I couldn't hear, and then turned her head away from me and I heard her breathing deepen.

I waited until I was out on the street before I called for a cab, and I met it by the McDonalds on the next block. I debated whether to have the driver take me straight home, but I had him drop me by my car instead. Mama's was still open, still doing business, but by the look of the parking lot it was for a different crowd.

The neighborhood was quiet when I finally reached home. The red light on the hallway machine was blinking, and when I ran the tape there was a message from Melissa.

"Hi, dad," it ran . . . *"Are we supposed to be coming to you this weekend or what? Mom wants to know. Call us back, thanks, byeee."*

I checked my watch. It was too late to call the house, but after I'd gone through into the kitchen and set some water to boil I got out my phone and fumbled out a text message with my thumbs on the keys. It took me about five minutes just to write *RU awake?* and less than a minute to get the reply from Melissa, *Yes but no $$ to call.*

So I called her cell phone, which I now knew would ring out in her hand and shouldn't wake the household, tempting though the prospect of that was. Rouse the new baby, and that would have been everybody up and cursing for an hour at least.

You might guess that I was having some problems with negative intimacy, and you'd be right. But I was doing my best to be aware of them. This meant that if I had a cruel thought, I could enjoy it more without feeling guilty.

"Hi," I said. "I got your message. Sorry it's late, I was out. What have you been doing?"

"Stayed in listening to Korn."

"Not too loud, all right?"

"Headphones, dad," Melissa said in that weary tone implying that I was an idiot and missing the obvious.

"Stop rolling your eyes at Tanya," I said.

"How do you know I'm rolling my eyes?"

I lied and told them I'd had a quiet evening catching up on paperwork at the office, thinking that I was justified in the context of all the bullshit they'd peddled to me in these teenaged years, and Melissa told me that they were bored out of their skulls and had made a blood pact never to have babies of their own.

I sympathized, told them that they could come home this weekend or any time, and that there was plenty of vacuuming and dusting for them when they got here.

The fact of it was that if I'd had my way, they'd never have gone back with Amy. I couldn't see the point of it. They were all but adults, and their friends and their lives were centered right here; the house in Alexandria was big, but it wasn't *that* big. Amy's sister would need the patience of a saint to juggle houseguests and a new baby, and I knew for a fact that she didn't have it. A short visit and a helping hand were one thing. But a needy sibling who insisted on toting along her rock-chick daughters for support in her crisis . . . if there were weapons in the house, I hoped they were under lock and key.

After the call I made the coffee, showered while it cooled, then wrapped myself in a ratty-comfortable robe and sprawled on the bed with the TV on and the unread sections of that morning's paper all around me. I did this mainly, I suspect, because I could, because I fell asleep with the coffee undrunk and the newspaper unread and the TV playing unwatched. I woke at about three, switched everything off, and got under the covers.

Then, of course, I lay awake.

It would be hard to say which was in more of a mess, the externals of my life or the inside of my head. I should have been pleased with myself right then, but I wasn't. I was single again and I'd just had more sex in one night than in the whole of the year so far. But I didn't know where I was going to live, or what my financial situation would be, or what new shape my personal life would fall into. It wouldn't just be a matter of adjusting to life without Amy. Everything was going to change.

Everything.

Tanya had told me that her mother had started styling herself Aimee since the split. I thought it was regrettable and slightly troubling, but I said nothing. To my mind it made her sound like some retarded child-woman out of a Tennessee Williams play. She said she wanted to assert her independence, which seemed to involve having other people acknowledge her needs while avoiding any obligations in return.

I must have lay there until at least four o'clock, turning stuff over in my mind. I couldn't take any of the pills because I'd been drinking, and I knew I'd rather stay on the rack than risk that kind of obituary. Loss might be there in my heart like a radioactive seed, but I wasn't about to let it get the better of me.

In the morning I'd go to the garden district, and I'd talk to the woman who'd given him the car.

EIGHT

WHERE THE Garden District of New Orleans is an entire section of the city and contains some genuine mansions, ours is mostly a wishful creation of the Chamber of Commerce and covers three or four blocks of Victorian housing. They're quaint, some of them are ivy-covered, and the streets on which they stand are broad and lined with mature trees whose roots break up through the sidewalks. One building is the town museum, the rest are all private homes.

I drove down one of the empty streets, looking for the address. New Orleans mansions might have more grandeur, but ours had more land and weren't squeezed together like dollhouses in a yard sale. Norma Lousteau's house stood at a corner on a rise, and I couldn't decide which it made me think of more, *Psycho* or *The Addams Family*.

One look at Norma Lousteau, and I could see why she'd been attracted to it. I'll bet she had every novel that Anne Rice ever wrote.

"Miz Lousteau?" I said, and showed her my identification. She glanced at it without much interest or enthusiasm.

"What is it this time?" she said.

"More of the same thing as last time, I imagine," I said. "Outside or in?"

I recognized the masks on the wall in the hallway. They were the same style as those in the Voodoo Gift Shop, which was probably where she'd bought them.

I followed her into the sitting room, which resembled a

Victorian parlor set up for a seance. But there was more than that. Over the ornate fireplace hung a painting of a saint and a peacock, done in a bright and primitive style, while along the mantel stood a row of dusty bottles. None of them was anything special, and no two of them matched. There was a handbell, a rattle, a bamboo flute. It wasn't just voodoo stuff, it was a weird pick'n'mix of ethnic decor. There were wooden carvings on side tables that looked like African souvenirs.

I didn't immediately see any cats, but you knew from the first breath that they were somewhere around.

"What now?" Norma Lousteau said. "It feels like I only just got rid of the others."

"They told you what your lodger's been doing?"

"Ex-lodger. He moved out. And none of what they told me was anything I could recognize as the truth."

Norma Lousteau herself was a solidly-built woman with kohl-ringed eyes and long dark hair so straight that it looked as if it had been ironed. It didn't look like a wig. On a young woman in might have been fetching in a gothic, Winona Ryder kind of a way; on a middle-aged woman it just looked batty.

I said, "He's a criminal on the run."

"You're making him into a martyr."

"How can you defend him?"

"There's a simple principle called freedom of worship. Some of us happen to believe in it."

"Miz Lousteau," I said, "you can worship anyone or anything you like." *And,* I thought, *by the look of it you do,* but I kept that to myself.

I went on, "We're not looking for him because we disapprove of his beliefs, except where those beliefs involve kidnap, extortion and attempted murder. You think these aren't serious matters?"

"A pack of lies, is what I think they are. No-one could show me a scrap of proof."

"What's his hold on you?" I said. "Tell me. I swear I'll do anything I can to help you break it."

But she was smiling sadly at me and shaking her head, in that *you-poor-child* way that makes you want to grab someone and strangle them.

She said, "He doesn't need a hold on me. I follow Legendre of my own free will."

"Legendre?"

"When a friend introduced me to him, he told me that I'd dream of a snake. And he was right, I did, I had exactly that dream, that very night. When I told him about it he revealed that my guardian lwa is Simbi, one of the snake gods." She gave a superior smile. To her that was QED, case proven. Test it with logic? You just don't understand. "Now, you tell me," she said. "How could he fake something like that?"

"He grabbed a child on camera in a shopping mall," I said. "He gave me a poison that all but killed me."

"He was risking himself to protect the boy."

"He told you that? So you've seen him since then."

After a moment she said, "You're very clever."

"I wish I was, but I struggle by. I want you to listen to me. If he contacts you again and you don't tell us, you become his accessory. If he does get in touch, don't give him anything and don't take him in. Just tell him this. We're on his trail and we don't plan to stop. We know his game, we know his methods, we know the kind of targets he looks for. We've found his money, and he can be sure that we'll stop him when he tries to get more."

Then I said, Tell him . . ." I trawled my memory for the exact phrase. "Tell him that someone is burning a candle against him."

"Don't try that," she said. "You'll lose. His will's stronger."

"We'll have to see," I said.

NINE

I WENT LOOKING for Dave Corrigan again but somebody told me that they thought he'd taken a couple of days off to visit his mother. I said to tell him that John Lafcadio had been asking. Whenever I looked for him he was always somewhere else, and I doubted that it was a coincidence. We were like two pieces in one of those tile puzzles where you slide them around in a frame, trying to put a picture back together.

To be honest, I didn't mind not finding him. I had nothing in particular to say. I was just enjoying the thought of him being in a constant sweat, watching for me and dodging out of the way.

Bob Lambert came by when I was at my desk.

"There's a problem with that chair," he said.

"I haven't noticed one."

"I have," he said. "Your ass is never in it."

Most of my workload involved follow-up contact with members of the public. Call and tell us that someone's kicked a dent in your car and, let's face it, there's not a lot we're going to be able to do about it . . . although I remember one complainant who'd made a precise record of time and location so we could contact the appropriate agency for spy satellite pictures of the thief taking the carp from his garden pond.

If only it worked that way. The most you'd better hope for is a report number for your insurance company and, if you're lucky, a call from someone like me to reassure you that you haven't been forgotten.

And then we all move on.

Meanwhile, the bocu and his entire arsenal of poisons could never diminish my will to live with as much success as this paperwork.

My phone rang between calls, and it was Frank Early.

"So what happened?" he said.

"I gave it a shot," I said, "but I got nothing from her."

"What, even after you left in a cab together?"

"What?"

"I'm talking about last night in the bar. What are you talking about?"

"My conversation this morning with the Queen of the Damned."

"Forget about her," Frank Early said. "We finally managed to get hold of Kenny Boudreaux' financial records. There's a document authorizing one Edward Vincennes to take cash directly from the company account, but it became invalid when Kenny Boudreaux became incapable and power of attorney passed to his wife by prior arrangement. Which will explain why Vincennes is pressuring her now. He wants restoration of his looting rights."

"Edward Vincennes? Is that another one of his made-up names?"

"It doesn't match with any database we've tried it on. But there is an arrest record for an Eddie Vinson that checks out against what little we know of our man's career."

"Eddie Vinson?" I said. "That's a long way from Legendre. He wouldn't have made it up. Would he?"

"It's a connection we're still trying to confirm," Frank Early said. "I faxed you his arrest pictures to see if anything jogs your memory. They should be with you by now."

"Wait a minute," I said. "Don't hang up."

I left the receiver on the desk and crossed the open-plan office to the shared fax machine, where the last half-dozen or so messages were in a tray and awaiting pickup and distribution. Surely I'd feel something if it really was him. Surely I would know.

We were supposed to be getting a network that would flash all this stuff direct to your desktop terminal, but the job had gone to someone's brother-in-law and it had been a disaster. The hardware was all in a room somewhere and had already fallen out of date.

Here it was. The fax scanner had made two solid black rectangles out of the pictures. You could just about glimpse the shape of a figure in one of them, like something lurking at the bottom of the Black Lagoon.

I scooped up the phone.

"These are no good," I said. "I'm coming over."

TRAFFIC WAS heavy and it took me more than half an hour to get there. I circled a couple of times until I saw someone pulling out of a slot, and then jumped into the space. I was right behind the bullet-pocked Mazda.

I felt all keyed-up. Life might be a shitstorm of turbulence and disorder, but this was a manhunt. It had meaning, it had purpose, and at its best it cut an ordered line through chaos. I could forget the bad stuff and focus. Everything else got pushed to the sidelines and priorities fell into order. It was the human drama in its leanest form.

As I was showing my ID to the desk man on the way in, an alarm buzzer went off on the panel under the counter and I could hear a bell ringing somewhere inside the building.

I asked him if there was some kind of a drill going on and he said, "Only the one that happens every time someone cracks open a fire door to save a two-minute walk, and I have to send a man down to reset it."

I left him canceling it off, and made my way through the building toward the hole-in-the-wall that was Cult Crimes Co-ordination.

It was the same mess as before, but with a few extras. Frank Early was slumped in his swivel chair, phone receiver in his hand, his hand down in his lap. The chair had been half-swung around and his brains were up the wall, still sliding down the laminated year planner.

Bram Shapiro was face-down on the floor, his back a mass of exit wounds. I got down beside him and I could see that he was drowning in his own blood. It was pooling under his face and he was snorting it in as he gasped for breath like a beached mackerel. I lifted him clear of it and shouted, "Bram! Hold on! You're going to be fine!" and he died in my arms. I don't think he even heard me.

I lowered him back to the floor and stood up. For a moment, I was thrown. If this was the street, I'd call it in. But this was the middle of the Fifth District building. It wasn't supposed to happen this way. I couldn't even pick up a phone—I didn't know any of the extension numbers.

Much as I didn't want to leave the scene, I had to. I ran down the corridor and threw open the first door that I saw. It was some kind of records office and my appearance stopped all conversation in an instant.

"Two fatalities," I said, "call your homicide people. Tell them someone's in the building, they just shot the voodoo cops."

I left them there with their mouths hanging open and ran all the way back to the front desk, where I warned the desk man to lock down the building and put on full security. He took one look at me and didn't argue. I looked down and saw that I had so much of Bram

Shapiro's blood on me that I looked like a victim myself.

When I got back to Cult Crimes I was ahead of the homicide people, but in the corridor just outside there was a crowd of civilian workers from the records office. They were looking stricken and concerned, and I said, "Please, go back, you can't help anyone here, this is a crime scene now."

They didn't disperse but they moved about ten feet down the corridor, and I went into the office and stood on the spot where I'd stood a minute or two before. I hadn't called for paramedics. Had I been wrong? After all, these were the men who'd pulled me back from the edge, and I owed them big-time.

But there was nothing subtle, ambiguous or open to interpretation about the state they'd been left in. They hadn't been drugged or hoodooed. They'd been visibly, physically destroyed. Without moving from my spot, I leaned a little for a better look at Frank Early. His head was a half-shell, a mask of a face with no back or side to the skull and a tiny entry wound just under his jaw. His entire head looked like a hollow bronze cast. Show me a paramedic who can turn back time, because that's the only thing that could have done it. The speed with which Bram Shapiro had bled out was a strong indication of an opened aorta. Cut the main pipe like that, and it comes out like a fire hose. The bullets through his heart and lungs were just unnecessary grace notes.

Homicide arrived on my heels. People who'd just put down their coffee and run.

They took it all in and breathed their dismay, and then one of them said to me, "Okay, what did you touch?"

"Just him," I told her, pointing at Bram Shapiro, and then I allowed myself to be led away while they got a grip on themselves and began to secure the scene.

My legs weren't entirely steady, now that I was starting to wind down. They sat me in a room and brought me some unsoiled clothing to change into, mostly borrowed from somebody's sports kit.

The woman I'd spoken to before came in and asked me, "What do you know? Do you know who could have done this?"

"I can't say anything about their other cases," I told her. "Just the one I was involved with."

I told her the story, and of how I'd come over to see if the arrest record of Edward Vincennes/Eddie Vinson promised to get us any closer to our target.

"What about a description?" she said.

"I've no memory of one," I said. "I'm sorry, I'm not bullshitting, it's one of the after-effects. I came over to look at his photograph."

They hadn't started moving papers yet, but she said I could go and that they'd contact me if they found anything. I went to the men's room and cleaned up a little more, then I went out to my car. They were checking people more closely than usual on the way out, but the lockdown had been lifted.

There was a white van in the space before me, and he'd squeezed in so tightly that I was going to have a tricky time getting out. He was inches from my bumper and there wasn't much clearance behind me. I had to shunt back and forth, swinging out a little further every time. I'd halfway done it, when a belated understanding dawned.

Instead of wasting more time putting the Jeep back into line, I left it as it was. I asked at the desk for the maintenance man who'd reset the door alarm, and when he arrived I had him take me there. The desk man was calling more questions after me but I didn't have time to stay and explain.

The emergency door had a crush bar with a fifteen-second delay and a notice that read DO NOT USE THIS DOOR AS A SHORTCUT TO THE STREET, ALARM WILL SOUND. I turned my arm so that I could press the bar with my elbow. The bolts withdrew with a bang, top and bottom, but an electronic lock held it shut while the alert bell rang out.

After fifteen seconds, the catch released and the door swung open. I found myself stepping out into the street that I'd just left. My car was about a hundred yards away. Looking back, I saw that the door when closed would seem like nothing more than a metal panel in the concrete with the usual graffiti sprayed on it.

When I stepped back inside, the maintenance man said, "What's the idea?"

"Don't touch the bar," I said. "Don't touch any other part of the door, and don't let anyone else touch it until it's been dusted."

"I already did," he said as I was moving away.

"Well, don't do it again!" I called back to him.

I went back to the scene. They were just getting ready to examine the bodies in situ. I spotted my homicide contact and waved her over.

"He's your man," I told her. "Vinson, Vincennes, Legendre, whatever name he goes by. You know how they'd impounded his car? It was right in front of mine when I got here, and now it's gone. Which means that someone was driving it away at the exact same time that I was finding the bodies. He must have got the keys from Bram Shapiro while he lay there."

"I don't get it," my Homicide woman said. "Car full of bullet holes, everyone knows it on sight. Why take the risk?"

"Because his money was hidden in it. If he's hoping that it hadn't been found, he's going to be disappointed."

She called her boss over, and they didn't waste any time. A team went down to dust the exit door and every police officer in town hit the street to look for the red Mazda with the perforated lid. They even got the local TV news helicopters in on it. I was out there myself, checking places like the garden district and the road that led out toward the Boudreaux house. I didn't think he'd go there, but I wondered if he might have a hideaway on one of those other big properties on that side of town. I saw nothing. After a while I drove back in, and I was cruising those dank and lightless parking areas under the elevated highway when my phone rang.

It was my Homicide woman.

"We've got him," she said.

"As in arrested, or just located?"

"There was a chase, but he couldn't cut it. As soon as he'd hit enough street furniture to kill the car, he jumped out and ran."

"Where is he now?"

"Third District are holding him. I'm heading over now."

"I'll see you there," I said.

TEN

"THAT ISN'T him," I said.

On the other side of the interrogation room glass sat a young black male in the standard-issue orange jail jump suit. I couldn't say whether he was co-operating or not. He certainly wasn't remaining silent. He was completely hyper, and when he talked he spoke so fast that it was hard to keep up with the words. They had a tape running and two Homicide officers asking the questions. One of the officers was Pete Lala, with whom I'd once worked. Someone from the Public Defender's office was sitting in as the young man's appointed lawyer.

Standing right behind me on the observation side, my Homicide woman said, "He was the only one in the car. There was a recently-fired gun under the seat and fresh blood all over his clothing."

"He may have done the deed," I said, "but he was sent by someone else."

I listened for a while.

"You can't scare me," the young man was saying. "You think you can make me promises? You're crazy. Nothing you can do about it. He thinks I'm talking to you, I'll die for sure."

"Who?" one of the detectives said. "Who are you talking about? Give me a name."

"He don't have a name. What are you trying to do to me?" He looked at his lawyer. "I tell you I don't want to talk," he protested, "and you let him keep asking me stuff."

"I've told you, you don't have to answer," his lawyer

said with a trace of weariness, as if he'd made the point about a dozen times already. "They can ask you the questions but if you don't want to say anything, don't say anything."

His client might not have wanted to speak, but his nerves were such that he still couldn't keep his mouth shut. They went on like this for a while, going in circles, and then Pete Lala appeared to lose his patience.

"Take a few minutes to think about your position," he said, rising to his feet. "None of this is helping you."

I left the observation suite and caught up with Pete Lala by the Coke machine outside.

"John!" he said. "I heard about your trouble."

"I'm still looking for the man behind it," I said. "That's why I'm here."

"How so?"

"I think your prisoner knows something that could help me. The problem is that he's more scared of whoever sent him than he is of you."

"I'll change that," Pete said.

"Believe me, that won't be easy. Can I have a couple of minutes with him?"

"I don't think so, John. You know the way it works."

"He killed the voodoo cops, there's a voodoo angle, I'm a cop and I'm also a voodoo victim. Are you telling me you can't see any point or sense in me talking to him?"

Pete thought about it. I could see that he was trying to think of a good reason to say no. But it wasn't as if he'd been making any progress on his own.

Finally, he checked his watch against the plastic clock on the wall. "I'm going back in five," he said. "I wanted to give his lawyer a chance to spell out his options. You think you can get anywhere?"

"Maybe."

"You have until then."

"Got a pen I can borrow?"

The young man's name was Maurice French. I checked before I went in. He was sitting alone with his lawyer, and they both looked up at me when I walked through the door.

I sat in the chair that Pete Lala had vacated. The main features of the room were its big veneered table and a green chalkboard on the wall; when not in use for interrogations, it was used for meetings. The lawyer was giving me a very puzzled look, partly because I'd come in unannounced but probably more because I was still in the mismatched sportswear that I'd borrowed. I must have looked like someone who pushed all his worldly goods around in a shopping cart.

I looked directly at Maurice and said, "I'm Sergeant Lafcadio, I'm a detective. Need a minute of your time. You don't have to speak if you don't want to. You can just listen." I nodded to indicate the mirror; there can't be anyone on the planet who doesn't know how those setups work or who thinks that the glass is just there for decoration.

I said, "They know you did it. The lab's going to match the bullets to your gun and the blood on your clothes to the victims. It doesn't matter to us whether you talk or not, it won't make a difference to anything."

The lawyer started to say something then, but I kept my eyes locked to Maurice's and talked across him.

I said, "But I know you're not entirely responsible. I know someone made you do it, and I know who that someone is. I know how he forced you and I know why. Who's your guardian lwa?"

I saw Maurice's eyes narrow. He knew what I was talking about.

"Don't tell me if you don't want to," I said. "Mine's Simba. Snake god."

I drew up the sleeve of my borrowed sweatshirt to reveal the crude snake on the inside of my arm.

"It's Simbi," Maurice said. "And what are you trying to pull on me? That's not a tattoo. You done it with a Bic."

"What makes you say that?"

"It's all smeared."

I looked, and it was. I should have let it dry off a bit more.

"Doesn't matter," I said, pulling the sleeve down again. "I'm making a point. You did what he wanted because he fixed you and now you're scared he'll fix you worse because you let him down. You killed the voodoo cops for him, but you didn't bring him the car and you got yourself caught. Am I right?"

There was silence.

I said, "He thought he'd fixed me, once. It didn't work. I'm still here."

Maurice sat back and folded his arms.

"No you ain't," he said.

A calmness seemed to have descended on him now, as of one who's just seen that his life has only one course and there's no point or purpose in any further anxiety about its outcome.

He said, "What you think you can offer me? Help and protection? Ain't enough cops on this planet can protect me now."

"I'll show you," I said.

PETE WENT back in to resume his questioning. I tried to call the Reverend Henry Zeno, first at home and then at the church, but both times the phone rang out and nobody picked up. So then I called Michael Zeno at the

Tire & Lube Express, and he told me that his father was at the Men's Mission.

The Gillespie Men's Mission was an old converted movie theater near to Dizzy Gillespie Park, after which it was named. I suppose it sounded better than the Dizzy Men's Mission, even though that wouldn't have been too far off the mark. It was a wedge-shaped building at the point where two streets met, with its marquee all smashed but still in place and its box office boarded up. Sponsored by a number of the local churches, the Mission provided beds for the homeless and a hangout for the aimless. Turned out at nine o'clock every morning, they'd wander across into the park and spend the day there. When the sun went down, they'd start to wander back and they'd camp on the sidewalk until the Mission doors opened again at eight.

When I got there, I found Henry supervising a small army of volunteers who were turning mattresses out onto the sidewalk to air in the low afternoon sunshine. They worked in teams of two, one to beat the ticking and the other waiting ready with a can of Raid to kill whatever ran out of it. Henry was in shirtsleeves, patrolling the ranks, leaning on his stick and offering the odd word of encouragement, taking care not to get too close.

"Henry!" I said. "Need your help."

He turned to me, just as I was regretting stepping out of the car. I should have dropped the side-window and called from there. The entire sidewalk smelled of piss and tobacco, and I suspected it was the kind of smell that would cling.

"To do what?" he said.

"You can help me stop a boy from living in fear. Our one-man white bizango's been using him as a messenger. Got him scared for his life."

"Is the boy in a safe place?"

"He's in jail."

He spotted something scuttling right in front of him, and lanced it accurately with the tip of his walking stick. "I got a lot to deal with here," he pointed out. "What did he do?"

"Less than two hours ago, he shot Bram Shapiro and Frank Early."

Henry stared at me, seriously. I can't always make out what his eyes are saying. You can't see into them, the way you can with most people. It can be like trying to read the emotion in a couple of pennies.

"They dead?" he said.

"They surely are. Bram died in my arms."

He waved for someone to bring his jacket.

"Then let's go," he said.

As I drove him back across town, he sat in the passenger seat of my car with his back straight and his hands folded in his lap like a maiden aunt on a buggy ride.

I said, "I can't tell him he's safe from danger, but he may believe it coming from you."

"It may be too late for that," the Reverend said.

"What do you mean?"

"If the boy's enemy has managed to get inside his head, what use is a man on the door?"

I'd been out of the building for less than an hour. Something had changed in that time. Pete Lala had abandoned his interrogation for the moment, and Maurice French had been taken to the holding tank. He'd been looked over by a doctor and given the all-clear.

I saw Pete in the corridor and said, "What happened?" But he simply shrugged and shook his head and waved me in the direction of the tank. We followed the prisoners' route over into the annex and took the elevator to the processing area.

For the second time that day I found myself being barred from entering a section of a police building that had been designated as a crime scene. But they let me take a look over the tape.

The cells in the holding tank were all bare, brutal, functional rooms from which every opportunity for self-harm had been eliminated. Because prisoners had been known to hang themselves from window bars, these had been replaced by dense glass bricks. There were no hooks or handles anywhere. Even the toilet flush was a two-inch conical button that you couldn't throw a loop over.

But Maurice had managed to prize off the conical button, and to hang himself by his underpants from the spindle onto which it had been fixed.

He was still in place. By which I mean, he was unhooked from the spindle and lying on the floor where they'd tried to revive him. They'd been checking every fifteen minutes and reckoned he'd been dead for ten when they found him.

I reckon they ought to show pictures of how a hanged person looks to every potential suicide. You'd think twice because there's no dignity in it at all. Everything lets go. You get a pumpkin head with bug eyes and a tongue like a salami. And the stink . . . well, let me put it this way. I once had the misfortune to visit an unventilated bathroom right after a fat man on a banana diet.

The stink from Maurice was almost as bad.

"You see what I mean?" the Reverend said. For a moment I'd forgotten that he was right behind me.

"I'm sorry you had to see this, Henry," I said. "Come on, I'll take you back."

I picked up the bag with my bloodstained clothing in it, and I drove the Reverend home.

That evening, after I'd showered and had a desultory flick through the trays of stuff in the freezer only to decide that no, I really didn't have any appetite, I did something that I can't recall ever having done before. I walked out of the neighborhood and a couple of blocks down the road to Lulu's, a workingmen's drinking hole with barstools like sawhorses and a confederate flag on the wall. I put some money in the jukebox and lined up three drinks on the counter.

One was for me, one for Frank Early, the other for Bram Shapiro. Men about whom I knew almost nothing. I didn't know what their homes were like, or if they had families. If they'd ever buried a well-loved pet or learned to ride a bicycle with an adult's hand on the saddle. I just knew the sound of their voices and the sense of their company and the fact that without their involvement, I wouldn't have been here now.

I was equally a stranger to them, and yet they'd saved my life. Now they were dead and I'd done nothing to prevent it. Worse than that, I had a queasy feeling that I'd somehow been the lightning rod who'd brought harm to them without suffering any permanent damage myself.

But that wasn't entirely true. They'd already been on the trail of the man who, even if he hadn't pulled the trigger, had authored their destruction. And as far as the lightning rod idea went . . . well, there's damage you don't see, and I was beginning to suspect that I had some of it. As the Reverend had more or less said, what use is all the external vigilance in the world if your enemy is inside your head? I was starting to believe that exotic Legendre or plain old Eddie Vinson had wormed his way into mine.

When the drinks were all gone I lined up three more, and when I was halfway through those I began to realize that even the first three had been a mistake on an empty stomach. I left the last untouched, put down money to cover my bill, and set out to walk back to the one place where I could throw up or fall over without fear of observation or disapproval.

The way it worked out, the walk home helped to clear my head and when I got there, I neither puked nor stumbled. I locked all the doors and put my gun on the coffee table and watched some TV, and didn't take in anything of what I saw. When the news came on, I changed channels. When the news was everywhere, I watched cartoons. I'd already seen far more of the day's events than I'd wanted to see.

For once, my sleep was dreamless. I think.

I awoke to the certain knowledge that I wasn't alone in my house.

ELEVEN

I HEARD MOVEMENT, I heard voices. I slid out of bed and moved in silence to the door so that I could listen. There was daylight coming through the drapes but I hadn't checked the time.

I could hear a woman.

I cracked the door about a quarter of an inch and put my eye to the gap. A moment later, I eased it shut and ran to get dressed. I got my foot caught in my pants leg and hopped around, terrified that the door would open and they'd catch me like this. I started straightening a few things in the room but by then I could hear them moving towards me, so I stepped out to meet them in the hallway.

Her name was Carol Shexnayder, and the couple with her had to be clients. She was the realtor whose sign was pegged into my front lawn. She was fortysomething with bubbly hair, heels, and a skirt that was just a shade too short for her. She had good legs for her age, but that's not the point. She usually wore an open-necked blouse with one of those chiffon neckscarves, knotted at the side. When we'd first met I'd been convinced that I'd never be able to remember her name, only to find that I could hardly get it out of my head.

She was surprised to see me.

"Mister Lafcadio!" she said. "I thought you'd be working."

"I ought to be," I said. "I'm catching up after a late one."

She turned to the couple beside her and said, "Mister Lafcadio is one of our police officers." They made approving faces, and little noises that weren't quite words.

He was short and kind of squinty, and she wore a polka dot tent.

"Don't let me slow you up," I said. "Please. Be my guests."

The deal was that she could have access with her own key during working hours but that she'd call me about any other time. I wondered what had gone wrong until I looked at my watch and realized that it was well after nine. I withdrew to our tiny second bathroom and left them to get on with it.

I washed in cold water and then ran some hot while I rummaged and found an unused razor in the cupboard under the basin. I realized that my presence was hardly the best sales aid and that the state of the place was none too entrancing either, but then it wasn't me who was in a hurry to sell.

There was a tapping on the bathroom door. "Mister Lafcadio?" I heard Carol Shexnayder calling. "Mister Lafcadio!" Quickly wiping my face, I opened the door.

She said, "Your lawn appears to be on fire."

I thought I'd misheard her.

"Excuse me?" I said.

So then she spelled it out, as if to an idiot. "The grass . . . behind the house . . . is burning. And a man appears to be dancing in it."

I went through the house. "Pardon me," I said as I squeezed past the bemused couple to look out of my kitchen window.

There weren't any flames, but there was a zigzag smouldering line across the grass in my yard. Johnny Dodds was there, trying to stamp it out before it could reach the garage.

I grabbed the aerosol extinguisher from the kitchen and went out to join him.

"I'm sorry about this, John," he said, stamping away to no great effect. "I'm going to put everything right."

"What happened?"

"Tryin' a few different things in the fry tank. Dropped in a quarter pig and the whole damn thing went over. The oil hit the fire jets, and here's what we got."

I started giving the aerosol a good shake and while I was doing it, I took a look over the fence. I could see the trail that the burning oil had left, snaking through one yard after another like a gunpowder fuse. At the far end of it, rising from Johnny Dodds' own property, there was a rising black column of smoke from the upset tank. His brother and the rest of his family were all there, trying to beat out the flames with blankets.

"Anybody hurt?" I said.

"Quarter pig don't look too healthy."

I pulled the yellow plastic tab on the fire extinguisher, pointed it, and pressed the cap. There was a *phhht* and a dribble of foam like a baby trying to spit, and that was it. I looked at the instructions to see if I'd done it right, and saw a use-by date of November 1999. Fortunately I could now hear the sirens of approaching fire trucks coming from a only few blocks away.

I said, "How'd it manage to run this far?"

"'Cause I tried to put it out with the hose."

"You did what? Don't you know what water does to an oil fire?"

"From experience, now, yes I do."

We needed to try something else. The lawn was still smoking like something out of *Apocalypse Now*. The fire crew would deal with it, but I didn't want it reaching the garage before they got here.

When I went back into the house, Carol Shexnayder was still pitching. You had to admire her tenacity, even though she was steadily having to raise her voice to compete with the sirens outside. She was pointing out how close to a Fire Station the neighborhood was in the event of an emergency.

"I'm sorry about that," I said. "Neighbor having a problem. Nothing wrong, though, they're all good people. 'Cept for the crack house on the corner. Hey. That's a joke."

I could see from Carol's face that I hadn't exactly made a conquest with it. She turned to the couple. "Is there anything else you need to see?" she said.

They were making those polite noises again and I said, "Well, if you'll excuse me," and tossed the useless extinguisher into the sink and grabbed an old towel from underneath it. I could hear Carol Shexnayder walking them back through the house as I ran water until the towel was soaked. I wrung the surplus out of it and then took it, dripping, out into the yard.

Johnny was still stamping around, still making no difference.

"Let's try this," I said, and spread the wet towel over a part of the smouldering ground. While Johnny was treading it in, I looked over the fence again. There were firemen all over his yard now, blasting everything with foam. Everyone who wasn't at work had turned out of their houses to watch. A dog was barking somewhere.

When I peeled up one corner of the towel, a gout of smoke and steam came out but the ground was no longer burning. We laid it on another patch and repeated the operation.

Johnny Dodds was still mortified.

"I'll sand it and bring you some seed," he said.

"Forget it, Johnny," I said. "They do this in the Amazon."

"Yeah?"

"Yeah, slash and burn. It grows back twice as good."

When I finally went back inside, I was expecting to find Carol Shexnayder gone. But she wasn't. She was waiting for me.

"Got someone else coming?" I said.

She said with a little tremor in her voice, "I am really angry with you, Mister Lafcadio."

I could guess why.

"Why?" I said.

"This isn't a game to me. This is my living. I don't like to feel that I'm wasting my time."

"Well, who does?"

"Do you want me to sell this house for you, or not?"

"I don't have any choice."

"And I don't have a hope in hell of finding a buyer when every time I come out here, I walk into something out of the Marx Brothers."

"Now, wait," I said. "It's not as if I laid this on."

"Last time it was a little girl ringing the bell to ask if I'd look after her dog for an hour."

"Well, that sounds hilarious."

"It doesn't make a good impression. And look at the place. Our agreement was that you'd keep it presentable."

She had me there. Comfortable, yes. Presentable . . . that depended on whether you thought that 'putting stuff away' took precedence over 'keeping stuff to hand'.

I said, "I was planning to tidy up last night. But I had an exceptional day yesterday."

"And how does that become my problem?"

My cell phone started to ring then. I couldn't remember where I'd left it, so I followed the sound through the house. Carol Shexnayder followed me, still talking.

"And pardon me for getting personal," she said, "but you live like you were raised by wolves."

"I've got your meaning," I said over my shoulder. "It's a mess. I'll have it cleaned up for next time."

"And can you let me know if you're going to be here? It helps if I can warn people."

My phone was with the clothing that I'd left in a heap last night. I'd intended to keep the soiled stuff and the borrowed stuff apart, but the bag had tipped over and some of it had spilled.

As I rummaged to find it, Carol Shexnayder said in a much-altered voice, "Is that blood?"

I saw that she was looking at the shirt I'd been wearing.

"Uh-huh," I said.

"Human blood?"

"Maybe some brains in there as well. Excuse me."

I straightened, thumbing the keypad just in time to prevent it from switching to the messaging service. I didn't recognize the incoming number on the little screen.

"I'm done here," Carol Shexnayder said, and the house echoed with the sounds of her hasty exit as I put the phone to my ear.

"Lafcadio," I said.

She didn't identify herself. But even though I wasn't expecting the call, I knew her voice right away.

"All right," Julie Boudreaux said, "you win. Let's talk."

She was breaking up a little and so I started to move back through the house to where the signal was better. I said, "Did something happen?"

"First thing I want to know is, am I speaking to a person or to a cop?"

"Believe it or not, it's possible to be both."

I was in the sitting room now, from where I could see that Carol Shexnayder was on my front lawn, struggling to uproot her sign.

Julie Boudreaux said, "If I'm going to take a risk it's got to be with a real human being, not some kneejerk with a badge. I just want you to know that if there was anyone else I could turn to, I would. So tell me, am I talking to you or am I talking to the police department?"

"Why do you feel the need to insult me?" I said. "If you want to talk to me, talk. If you don't, just hang up."

"Okay," she said resignedly. "Come out to the house. I can't take any more of this."

TWELVE

I DIDN'T EVEN have to get out of my car at the gate. She must have been watching the security monitor for my approach. I slowed for as long as it took the gate to roll open, and managed to drive straight through without actually stopping. Even so, I'd had time to note that someone had spraycanned some red graffiti on the speakerphone box.

There was no sign of the dogs. When the house came into sight I saw that the vandalism had extended to within the compound, to the house itself. There was more graffiti up on the deck level, sprayed across the white stucco and onto the glass of the windows. Most of the painted designs seemed to involve hearts and snakes. It didn't take a great leap of the imagination to guess what they were.

I went up. She was waiting.

"When did all this appear?" I said.

"During the night," she said. "The dogs were out, but they never made a sound."

"Where are the dogs now?"

"I don't know. I wasn't about to go looking."

I studied the nearest design. This one looked like it was meant to be a cross on top of an altar with little coffin-shapes all around it.

"Did he get into the house?" I said.

"I don't think so. I haven't seen any sign of it."

"Hard to imagine he'd get in and not leave the same kind of mark."

"I know they're voodoo symbols, but I don't know what they mean."

"They could mean something, or he could have made them up. It doesn't make any difference. It's just scare tactics."

"There's a lot more to it than that."

"He doesn't have any special powers, Miz Boudreaux."

"Easy enough for you to say. You don't know him like we do."

"What he has is a monkey grip on your psychology and a bag of criminal tricks to back it up." I looked out across the unprepossessing land surrounding the house. This was what you got when you cleared the natural growth and then did nothing with it.

I said, "How do you get the dogs in?"

"With a little remote the trainer gave us. You press a button and it makes a sound. Only dogs can hear it. I've been trying it all morning, but the dogs don't come."

"Go inside," I said. "Lock your door if it makes you feel better."

I didn't think he'd still be around. But he'd made her nervous enough to want to talk to me, which I counted as progress. It wouldn't hurt if she stayed nervous for a while. Once she was safely inside, I walked out across the bare ground to where the undergrowth began. I scanned the ground as I went, but I saw nothing of interest.

Yesterday had been a good news/bad news day as far as our man was concerned. He'd succeeded in eliminating his pursuers with no risk to himself. The bad news was that he'd failed to retrieve his money.

I don't think I'd been any part of his calculations at all.

With the day's business out of the way, it looked as if he'd swung his attention back to the matter of screwing new cash out of his most likely prospect. He was broke once again, and this invasion of security would be the first softening-up move in a renewed campaign to scare up more payments.

Julie Boudreaux's problem was that from what I'd seen, scared or not, there didn't appear to be much left.

By following the fence around on the inside I found the dogs at the furthest extent of the property, by a kind of dry gully where the land fell away. The gully had been blocked with posts and wire, and two of the posts had been pulled out of the ground to make a space where a body could crawl through.

The dogs were lying on the ground, sleek but still, a couple of slate-blue quotation marks against the raw dirt. They looked dead to me. Their eyes were open and dry and there was a dried-out patch of something yellow and sticky under each muzzle. But just to be sure, I took out my gun and, standing over them, I shot each of them, once, in the head.

Then I went back to the house.

"I heard shots," she said, so I explained.

"I don't think he'd waste his zombi powder on a couple of dogs," I added. "He probably just threw some poisoned meat over the wire. I think they were dead, but for their sake I was making sure. I'm no voodoo cop. If they weren't, there's nothing I could do to help them."

We were in her big empty sitting-room with its bare floors and its walls stripped of art. Christopher Boudreaux was sitting on the couch, watching us, saying nothing.

Julie Boudreaux was shaking her head. "I have to get away from here," she said.

"Where do you want to go?"

"I don't care. Anywhere he can't reach us, if there is such a place. Can you help me do that?"

"Right after you tell me how you got into this situation, and what he wants from you."

"I'll tell you everything when we get there."

"I don't think so."

I sat down.

I could see her wondering what she'd missed, running the last few lines through her mind, looking for the processing error.

"Why not?" she said.

"Because by then you'll have what you want, and you'll just close up on me again."

Now she understood.

"I might have known," she said. "You're a bastard on the same scale that he is."

"Yeah," I said, "but maybe not so high on it."

She sent Christopher upstairs to pack himself a bag of clothes.

"I can't do it all on my own," he protested, but she told him to go on up and make a start and that she'd take over in a while.

Then when Christopher was out of earshot, she sat down and told me the story.

Kenny Boudreaux ran the kind of business that I wish I could understand, the kind where you own nothing and make nothing but you can still get rich. He dealt in land development, taking an option on some unpromising piece of scrub or swamp and then enhancing its value with plans and permissions before selling it on. It involved a lot of schmoozing, a lot of contacts in city and state politics. A lot of doing stuff for people who can do stuff for you. Ever wondered why that strip mall struggles in the middle of nowhere, why there's a marina with no boats in it? Someone like Kenny needed a second Lexus, is the probable reason.

As with any line of business, there was a subculture of these people who both competed and fraternised with each other. One golden couple had Kenny itching to know their secret. The deals were always bigger, the projects always more ambitious, the rewards always greater. Kenny moved in. The men played golf while the wives traded feng shui tips, and eventually the shoulder-rubbing paid off. Just occasionally, the little guy has something that the big guy needs. In exchange for a certain phone number, Kenny got an introduction to the big guy's Vodoun consultant.

Kenny was dubious at first. He didn't say it to his wife but it was clear that, to his mind, behind every Western businessman with a feng shui'd office stood a trophy spouse with too much time on her hands. Channeling the natural forces to enhance one's affairs? Yeah, okay, look, whatever you like, just get on with it and let me make this call.

But it sounded as if, as time went by, Kenny was the one to be won over.

She said, "Things started to happen. Things you just couldn't account for. Not unless there were . . . I don't know what else you can call it, *forces* working on your behalf. Things that had no reason to go our way . . . suddenly they did."

"Like what?" I said.

"We'd been having some trouble over a boy at Christopher's school. It ended, just like that. Deals went Kenny's way for no obvious reason. Doors he thought he'd have to push at, they just opened."

"How long did that last?"

"Hard to put a time on it. Six months? I don't know. We started to take it more seriously then. Kenny got more into the different spirits and stuff and I redid the house and made us an altar."

"So how did it start to go wrong?"

"Kenny came home one time, white as a ghost. He

went straight into the bathroom and threw up. He was trying to get a deal on this parcel of real estate outside of town, you know on the ferry road where the old quarantine hospital stood? But one of the Aldermen was petitioning the state for a highway extension that was going to cut through the land. Well, two hours before the appeal, the Alderman was found dead in his car."

I could remember it. "Natural causes?"

"Heart failure."

We'd been involved because the outward circumstances had seemed suspicious—dead in his car, side of the road, no medical history—but we hadn't found anything to back those suspicions up.

"You don't believe it," I said.

"Kenny didn't," she said. "I mean, it happens. People die. But I think there was stuff that Kenny hadn't been telling me about and this was just the last straw. He said, that's it with Legendre. He talked about a deal with the devil, getting a tiger by the tail. But the next morning, it was business as usual and he told me to forget everything he'd said. Five weeks after that, I was signing the papers to get him into hospital. He was going to all his meetings, but he was just sitting there crying and crying."

"How is he now?"

"Oh," she said with ill-disguised bitterness, "he's fine where he is. Out of reach, everything off his shoulders. And suddenly I'm here with responsibility for a business that's had everything leached out of it, debts like you couldn't imagine, and—get this—a set of accounts that had no other purpose than to convince Legendre that the corpse he was sucking on had life and blood and eternal riches to spare."

"Kenny didn't want to risk his bocu getting angry?"

"Kenny was going down in flames. But Kenny found an

escape route. I hope the nurses are spitting in his raisin bran. Once Kenny was out of the way, Legendre turned his attention to me."

"Let me guess," I said. "You told him the truth, and he wouldn't believe you."

"Of course he wouldn't. He'd seen the books, hadn't he?"

I couldn't help noting that the name he was using here was the one that he'd dropped for getting laughed at in California. Maybe he thought it would play better amongst the less sophisticated. Which I felt was an insult. On the other hand, it was a peek into his personal fantasy that made him a degree less intimidating.

Legendre. I mean, come *on*. I said, "So what happened then?"

"He started making threats," Julie Boudreaux said. "Veiled ones. He never says anything straight out. He made a point of mentioning Christopher."

"This is serious stuff, Julie," I said. "You really ought to come in and put it on record."

"No!" she said.

"Why not?"

"Because whether you believe in him or not, he can do what he says he will!" She got to her feet and looked down on me.

"I've told you the story," she said. "Now it's your turn to deliver. Take me somewhere safe. I know you must have places. If I could give him what he wants, I'd do it. But I don't have that option, and he won't believe me."

I was doing pretty well with her. I felt that if I could keep up this momentum, I could do even better.

"Okay," I said. "Pack an overnight bag and I'll see what I can do."

I asked if there was a shovel anywhere, and she gave

me the keys to the garage down below. In there I found a black BMW and a silver Mercedes, side by side. At the back I found a boy-sized dirt bike, a full set of gardening equipment, and handwritten work roster in Spanish with its last date around three months before.

I took the shovel and went off to bury the dogs. Christopher came out and followed me, at a distance. This didn't strike me as a good idea. He wouldn't come close enough to speak but when I tried to wave him away, he just stopped and waited until I was done and then came on as before.

They were exactly as I'd left them. I called them Catahoula curs but their proper name is the Catahoula Leopard Dog, an animal with a dash of red wolf and about four other breeds in its ancestry. They're not bred to be mean, just protective. I walked around, probing the ground with the shovel, all the way down into the gully until I found a patch of dirt that seemed a little softer than the rest, and there I started to dig. I wasn't going to make this deep. Just enough to plant them decently and cover them over.

Christopher stood on the lip of the gully, looking down at me.

"Don't watch if it upsets you," I said.

"It doesn't bother me," he said. "They killed my chinchillas."

I took a break, and leaned on the shovel.

"How'd that happen?" I said.

"First night we had the dogs, they dug into the pen. Didn't eat them or anything. Just killed them and left them for me to find."

"Want to help me cover them over?"

"Not really."

"Okay," I said, "don't strain yourself."

I dragged them to the shallow pit by their feet, and threw the dirt back into the hole. I'd have covered the grave with stones had there been any, but I saw none. There was sweat in my eyebrows and my shirt was sticking to my back when I climbed out of the gully with the shovel in my hand. I couldn't quite keep my footing and I don't think I cut much of a figure. As I started back toward the house, Christopher fell into step beside me.

"I heard about your trouble at school," I said.

There was no response to that, so I went on, "Legendre got you out of it? Any idea how he did that?"

"He gave me some Get Away Powder," Christopher said. "Told me to put it in Jimmy Nolan's food and he'd leave me alone. It was easy enough to do. I just put it on the stuff in my lunchbox and watched him take it from me like he always did."

"What happened?"

There was a silence for a moment and I thought he wasn't going to answer me, but when I glanced at him I saw that he was looking at the ground in front of him and seemed to be enjoying the picture in his mind.

He looked up at me and grinned.

"He still isn't right," he said.

When we got back to the house I saw that Julie Boudreaux's 'overnight bag' consisted of four pieces of airline luggage lined up on the second-floor deck, plus a more colorful tote bag of her son's. She was locking the house behind her.

Looking up at the lined-up set, I said, "Are you sure you've packed enough to scrape by?"

"Don't be funny," she said.

They were heavy, too. On the first trip down to the car, I tried to carry two of them. The others I brought down one at a time. As we drove out, they both sat in the back like I was their chauffeur. The gate was open when we reached it. She dialled a number on my phone to trigger a signal from the house to close and lock it, which was something that I'd never seen before.

"Where are you taking us?" she said.

"I'm still thinking about that," I told her.

About half an hour later, I was pulling over to the curb and stopping the engine. We'd arrived.

There was a conspicuous silence from the back and then she said, "What do you call this?"

"Temporary accommodation," I said.

I heard her breathe a word that she probably wouldn't have wanted her son to hear, had it been said by anyone else.

"What's the matter?" I said.

"Isn't this the ghetto?"

"No, it isn't," I said testily. "It's my house."

Well, what else could I do? This was all unofficial and I had no other ideas.

She said, "I thought you had safe houses, witness relocation, things like that."

"Miz Boudreaux," I said, "I work for the Iberville Police Department. We don't even have a Coke machine that gives you change."

I got out of the car, and dug around in my pocket for my keys.

"Don't forget to bring your bags," I said, and started up the path.

THIRTEEN

IT WAS late in the day, but I reckoned it would still be worth trying to get in to see Kenny Boudreaux. He was the one who'd been closest to our self-styled bocu, and he was the one who'd dealt with him on a daily basis.

I left Julie Boudreaux and her son to get settled in while I set out for the St Francis Center. After that first, unimpressed reaction she'd attempted to conduct herself with better grace, and had come close to managing it. I'd opened up the folding bed for her, which was how we turned the box room into a guest room, and I'd put Christopher into the girls' room. I told them not to answer the phone if it rang. I doubted that I'd be seeing Carol Shexnayder again—there was now just a hole in the lawn to show where her sign had been—but I warned them about the slim possibility of running into her.

The St Francis Center was a former Catholic boarding school on the north side of town. It had been built in the nineteen-twenties and run down almost to dereliction in the nineteen-sixties. I think it had then stood empty for a few years before being bought, converted and extended on the cheap. As I stood in the tiled entrance hall, waiting for the duty psychiatrist to come down and okay my visit, I noted that it smelled of floor wax and bodily fluids. The duty psychiatrist, when he appeared, looked like a man who was moonlighting from some other, more prestigious position.

Kenny Boudreaux was a surprise. I hadn't seen a picture of him, but I suppose I'd unconsciously formed one in my head. While Julie Boudreaux was taut and bony and their son was a slight little thing, Kenny wasn't tall and yet must have weighed around two hundred and fifty pounds. I'm not talking wobbly fat, I'm talking slab-of-beef construction. He was sitting in front of the TV, alone in a room with a dozen empty chairs in it. On the TV was a Tarzan movie.

"Mister Boudreaux?" I said, showing him my badge. "I'm John Lafcadio."

He glanced at the ID and then he turned his head to look up at me and his expression was neither unwelcoming nor unpleasant, but he said, "You know I can have you thrown out of here."

"For what?" I said.

"Compromising my treatment," he said. "I took advice after that visit from the last two."

I lowered my voice and leaned close to him. "Mister Boudreaux," I said, "I'll be very surprised if you're getting any treatment that's worth the name. Your wife can't afford it and you don't deserve it."

He looked pained.

"That's uncalled for," he said, but still his good humor seemed undiminished. I wondered if there was some chemical regulator at work in his system, pumping the happy pedal.

"You're right," I said. "I apologize." And then I pulled over one of the empty chairs and sat down.

He said, "What do you want, detective?"

"I want him," I said. "Out of circulation, off the market, incommunicado. You know who I'm talking about. I don't care how I do it and I think you could give me some leads."

He gave a good-natured shrug. "It's not gonna happen," he said.

"Why not?"

"Because I know who you are and I heard what he did. He got you. You're his zombi now."

"Don't give me that 'Oh, he's too powerful' crap," I said. "I don't believe it, and I don't believe you believe it. Do you know what I really think? I think that maybe your being here is just a scam on the scammer."

"That doesn't make any sense," he said.

"No?" I said. "I think it does. It could be that the real money's safe somewhere and you're planning to crawl out of your hole when the conflict ends. Warring parties in pieces all over the battlefield and you sneaking through the carnage with a satchel of cash."

He seemed unoffended. "You don't have one scrap of hard evidence for that," he said.

"Maybe not," I said. "But what do you think's going to happen if I let him think that I do?"

I saw the first hint of a frown.

"What do you mean?" he said.

"I just can't get my head around the thought of someone who'd create a situation like this and then dodge out of it, leaving his wife and kid to take the pressure. What kind of a man are you?"

"You can't do this," he protested. "I'm a hospital patient, for Christ's sake."

"Give me something I can use, and I'll go."

"I don't know anything."

"How can I find him?"

"You don't. He finds you."

"I can put the idea around. The minute he gets wind of it, he'll be up here like a dog after a bird. You think you've got him off your back? Think again."

Boudreaux moved as if to frame a reply.

And then, in a way that I'd never seen a human being react before, he simply fell apart before my eyes.

It was the way that a building falls when you blow its foundations out, so smooth it was almost graceful. He seemed to drop in his seat. His chin started to tremble and then his face screwed up and then he was bawling like a three-year-old.

If it was an act, it was better than good. But I didn't think it was an act.

I went over and pulled the cord that rang the staff buzzer. A male nurse took a long time coming and when he arrived, he didn't exactly rush in. He stood there, looking at Kenny Boudreaux for a few seconds, and then he looked at me.

"What happened?" he said.

"I wish I could tell you," I said. "He just cracked up."

"What did you say?"

"Nothing."

Kenny was red-faced, as if his own tears were scalding him, and there was stuff blowing out of his nose.

The male nurse crouched down beside him and brought all of his professional expertise to bear on the situation.

"Kenny," he said. "You stop that, now. You hear?"

There was nothing I was going to learn, so I left them to it. I'm sure I could have handled him better, but I'm not sure how. It was as if Eddie Vinson had sucked his soul and left nothing but a shell. When I'd poked at the shell, it had caved right in like something rotten.

My car was on the gravel turnaround in front of the building. Naturally I felt bad, but I was fairly detached about it. It doesn't help to be otherwise, when faced with a victim. They're damaged, it's done, you have to look ahead for them. If they scream a little when you probe their wounds, it's just a necessary part of the treatment.

On the way home, remembering that my guests would

need to be catered for, I stopped at a supermarket and picked up some packs of spaghetti and jars of sauce. With Christopher in mind I went into the freezer section and added a pack of Turkey Dinosaurs, and on my way to the checkouts collected extra breakfast cereal and milk.

The perfect host, I thought. Any complaints, and I'd have to say that Pennywise had been out of truffles and *foie gras*.

But I needn't have bothered because when I reached the house, every window was dark and there wasn't a single sign of life anywhere about the place.

I let myself in and walked through, checking all the rooms. Their bags were gone, so nothing suspicious about it; even the most committed kidnapper would have drawn the line at so much haulage.

So I set down the grocery bags in the kitchen and reckoned that I had a right to feel offended. This was not the ghetto, nor was my house a slum. It wasn't pretty-perfect but let's face it, I wouldn't have wanted to live in most places that were. Just look at the people who do.

Someone rang the doorbell and when I went to answer it, I found Johnny Dodds standing there. In his hand was a sinister-looking lump of something wrapped in foil.

Apparently he'd been watching the house for my return.

He said, "She called a cab and went off in it. Took all her suitcases like she wasn't coming back."

"When was that?"

"While you were out. It . . . *could* have been my fault."

"Why?"

"Honest to God, John, I didn't realize you had visitors. I rang your bell and no-one answered, so I was leaving this outside your door and I looked up and saw her looking scared at me through the window."

I looked at what he was holding up. It had the size and weight of a mis-shapen baby's head, and there was a bone sticking out of it. Around the bone was a bow of colored ribbon.

"What is it?" I said.

"A piece of the quarter pig. By way of apology. For, you know, doing the rain forest thing to your lawn."

"I told you to forget about that. And I thought the quarter pig was ruined."

"It came up okay with a scrape'n' bake. We kept some and gave the rest to the church."

Now he explained it, it was obvious. Almost.

"Is that the gift wrapping?" I said of the bow.

"Had that left over from Christmas," Johnny said. "Have I messed up something for you, John?"

"No, Johnny," I said. Johnny Dodds was an alarming enough sight to find outside your window, and it was conceivable that the piece of quarter-pig had the look of a voodoo sacrifice or a burnt offering.

I said, "She's had some bad experiences you couldn't know about. I don't suppose you remember which cab company she used?"

"Just that it was like one of those airport limos. That was a lot of bags for one woman and a kid."

After I'd sent Johnny away, I went to the phone and hit the redial button and found myself talking to Alpha Cabs, probably the first company in the Yellow Pages. I identified myself as a police officer and had them check the ride. I had their destination in less than a minute.

A minute after that, I was talking to her.

She couldn't quite believe it. "How did you find me?" she said.

"Anyone could reach you just as fast," I told her. "Next time, at least register under a different name."

"Can I do that and still use my credit cards?"

"Stay where you are. Don't go out. I'm coming right over."

They'd gone from here to the Ambassador Suites Hotel, which was sited next to a business park by one of the interstate off ramps. It was new, neat, anonymous, bland . . . scratch the wood or the gilt, and underneath it's all plastic. If that's your idea of luxury, then they're luxurious. They're more like short-let serviced apartments than hotel rooms, and they're mostly used by the technology companies for their contract workers.

I drew up in their well-lit but almost-empty parking lot with the interstate roaring by overhead like a party heard from the other side of a hill. The few cars there all looked like rentals.

So, no flophouse or budget motel for *this* lady. I've noticed before how some people's idea of being flat broke seems to differ from mine. It never seems to slow down their spending or make them lower their standards. They still show up in the same restaurants, and wouldn't ever consider giving up their designer labels for chain store goods. The part I can never understand is how they get away with it.

There was minimal front-of-house, just one man behind a desk and not another living soul in sight. I told him that Mrs Boudreaux was expecting me. He told me where to find her.

I rode up in the elevator to the muffled sound of Mozart, and stepped out into a corridor of regency stripes and chandeliers.

The door to the room wasn't properly secured. I knocked and no-one came, so I pushed it open. As I went in I could see that the thick carpet had slowed its closing and left it with insufficient force to make the lock.

It wasn't so much a suite of rooms as one big room with separate areas. I found her in the main sleeping section.

She was stripped naked on the king-sized bed, lying on top of the covers, pale and immobile and cold as a stone.

FOURTEEN

I'VE SEEN some sights, but this wasn't one I'd been expecting. It stopped me in my tracks for a moment while my mind raced to catch up. I'd been speaking to her on the phone . . . how long ago? The way my thoughts were spinning right then, I couldn't even work it out.

I made an effort and took control. The first thing that I did was drop to one knee beside her and check for a pulse. I couldn't detect one.

Then, quickly, I looked through the rest of the suite for some sign of Christopher. He wasn't there, not even hiding in the bathroom. I went back to the bed and threw all three sides of the cover over her like a tortilla wrap, and then I dropped to my knees again and took her face in my hands so that I could turn her dead eyes to look right into mine.

"Julie," I said. "I know you can hear me. I know what he did. Don't be scared, you're going to be okay."

I laid her head down carefully and then reached for the phone. It was then that I became aware of a cloth-wrapped bundle alongside it on the bedside table.

As I was calling the hospital, I picked the bundle apart one-handed and with some care. It looked like a piece of an old shirt. There were about half a dozen different things in it. I saw a small piece of rock, an eyedropper bottle full of fluid, various twists of paper with different-colored powders in them. It occurred to me belatedly that touching this stuff with my bare hands might not be the best idea.

"County General Hospital. This is Marcy speaking.

How may I help you?"

It took a couple of minutes to establish that the doctor I wanted to get hold of wasn't there. She was off-duty and couldn't be reached. Her name was Jody Fitzgerald. She was the one who'd finally listened to the voodoo cops and followed their advice on reviving me, and she was the only member of the medical profession I could rely on not to kill this patient with well-meant but inappropriate treatment.

I still thought of myself lying there while those paramedics came toward me with their defib paddles. A real ball-shriveler of a memory if ever there was one. I could get some different doctor and stand over them with a gun, but I couldn't then tell them what they needed to do.

"Thanks, Marcy," I said. "I've got someone else I can try."

I made another call.

When that was done, all I could do was wait.

Well, maybe not quite all. I straightened her legs out and arranged the bedcovers better to keep in what little body heat she had. Then I took hold of her face again and said, "You're not going to die. You're just all slowed down. I'm going to blow some air into your lungs so you'll get more oxygen."

With her head tilted back, I pinched her nose shut and then covered her mouth with my own and blew in some air. Her chest rose suddenly, and even though I'd known it would happen the shock of it made me start back. Slowly, the new breath rattled out of her. Then I did it again.

Is this how I'd looked to the world? God Almighty. She looked, felt, she even tasted dead. Only faith and experience kept me believing otherwise. I paused for a moment, lightheaded with the effort. I held her with her cheek resting on my hand, while her eyes were fixed and staring right past me.

Over the next half-hour I kept this up at the rate of a couple of breaths every minute. I kept checking for a pulse in between, hoping that I'd maybe catch that one elusive beat, but I felt nothing. I even started to wonder if a subtle trick was being played on me. That this was a double-bluff, and actually she was as dead as she looked.

Fooled you.

Made you jump.

But that didn't make any sense. A dead woman couldn't pay. A deeply scared and traumatized one . . . well, that was another matter. I kept her going, talking to her in between times, pacing my own breathing so that I didn't get dizzy. When the phone finally rang, I still hadn't seen anything like a flicker from her.

It was the desk clerk, and he was sounding dubious.

"There's a man here who's claiming to be on police business," he said.

"I know who he is," I said. "Send him up."

There was a tap at the door about a minute later. I opened it and let in Freddie Small, owner and manager of Iberville's one and only Voodoo Gift Shop.

He had a tote bag over his shoulder and he came in looking furtive, like he expected to be grabbed by the collar and slung out at any moment. "What have we got?" he said, and I led him through the suite to where Julie Boudreaux lay on the bed.

"Anything new happen since you called me?" he said.

"Not a thing," I said. I explained that I'd covered her over, but otherwise she was just as she'd been when I'd found her. I said, "The boy was gone and that stuff was there on the table. I believe she's still alive and that this entire stunt is meant to scare her and send me a message."

He set the tote bag down beside the bed.

"Let's take a look," he said, and crouched to unzip it.

First he took out a couple of fresh latex gloves, and snapped them on like a professional. I felt the way you do when your car's stranded you somewhere and the breakdown service finally shows up and gets to work. He reached over and felt at her neck.

"You won't find a pulse," I said. "I didn't."

He tried for a while anyway, then made a face and turned his attention to the bundle on the bedside table. Instead of just picking over it as I had, he spread the cloth right out and started opening the packages it contained. Some held powders as I'd thought, but one contained dried roots and the biggest had a shriveled lemon in it.

"I know what most of these are," Freddie Small said. "That one does nothing. That's just salt." He picked up what I'd thought was a white rock, and touched it to the tip of his tongue. "Yep. Salt."

I said, "If you're going to do that, where's the point in wearing the gloves?"

Freddie looked up at me.

"Make some allowances," he said. "This is all new to me too."

"Oh, great," I said. "I thought I was bringing in the expert."

"Don't worry," Freddie said. "I've got someone I can call."

As he pulled out his phone and worked the speed-dial one-handed, I said, "Who?"

"My cousin Kate. She's in anesthesiology at Dukes." He indicated Julie Boudreaux's inert form. "Best if you keep blowing her," he said to me and then, leaning in and tilting his head at an awkward angle to get himself on her eyeline and address her directly, added, "If you'll excuse my choice of expression."

I went back to work. First he tried his cousin's number, but her phone wasn't switched on. Then he tried a different number that got him through to a switchboard, from where he had them page her. It didn't exactly feel like a promising start.

As we waited, Freddie said, "You got two basic theories on what makes up a zombi poison. One says it's a bacterial agent called tetrodotoxin. The other's a plant extract, you get it from Jimson Weed. Or there's three theories if you count the one that says it's all bullshit and there's never any such thing."

"Never mind the theories," I said between exhalations. "What about an antidote?"

"For tetrodotoxin there isn't one. That's the same thing as the blowfish poison that kills you if you go to Japan and choose the wrong place for dinner. It also comes in crabs, snails, frogs, and an amphibious lizard over in California where your boy started his career. Your only treatment is to support the breathing and keep the heart going until it wears off. It blocks the sodium channel in nerve tissue. That means there's no electrical impulses can get around the central nervous system. Binds on in six different places, no messing around. But it doesn't cross the blood-brain barrier, so your consciousness isn't affected. You can watch 'em burying you."

"Yeah, or worse," I said. At least he seemed to know his subject. "You think it's that?"

"I don't know," he said. "That stuff takes a while before it kicks in. Twenty minutes before you feel the effects, and then it can be hours before you get the total paralysis. You were already looking dead when they reached you."

"And she was talking to me on the phone barely half an

hour before I got here. What about the other kind?"

"Datura stramonium. In Haiti they call it the zombi's cucumber. It's a hallucinogen, causes a kind of stupor. Scrambles your brain, keeps you confused. There's a natural antidote to that one, physostigmine. For the fish poison they reckon that atropine can help fight it, but I don't know. Whatever it is he uses, I don't think it's just one pure thing. I need to talk to Kate."

She came on then, and he quickly explained the problem. "Can you call me back?" he said. "This is costing me a friggin' fortune."

His cousin must have been moving to some more suitable place for the conversation, because it was at least a couple of minutes before Freddie's phone rang again. He waved me aside as he listened, and I scrambled out of his way as he took my place by the bed.

I was feeling pretty wrung-out by now. Rather than hover, I went through into the sitting-room part of the suite. Two couches faced each other across a coffee table in front of a fake fireplace. They were buttoned plastic, meant to look like leather. They were like the carpet, which was deep enough to leave footprints but made of some coarse artificial fiber in a shade unknown to nature. The pattern of marks in it suggested there had been a struggle, but I couldn't read the situation in any more detail than that.

I took out my phone and made a couple more calls but after that it was no use, I couldn't settle away from the action. I went back to watch. Freddie was saying, "Yeah, there's the fixed pupils and apnea. How the fuck would I know about brain stem reflexes? I'm in a hotel room."

As far as I could make out, Freddie and his cousin were testing the idea that the bundle might have been left as some kind of revival kit. He'd taken some bottles with handwritten labels out of his bag, and he seemed to be using those to run tests on the powders. The roots, the lemon and the rock salt had all been placed to one side. He had reagents and indicator papers. Every now and again he'd take a swab and apply a touch of something to the inside of his patient's cheek, and then he'd watch her for a while and report on what he saw.

At one point, he turned to me.

"Kate's got a question for you," he said, so I put my hand out for the phone.

"Hi, Kate," I said. "This is John Lafcadio."

"I know who you are," she said. "I've been reading all about you."

"What in?" I said. "Voodoo Monthly?"

"Scientific American," she said. "You got a name check on the news page. I need to know this. When you were affected and you finally came around, how did you feel?"

"You mean like, apart from relieved?"

"How long between getting movement back and standing up, walking around?"

"I don't know," I said. "It was pretty fast when it happened. I felt shitty at first, I slept like the dead for twelve hours, and then I was more or less okay."

"And how quick did it come on?"

"Couldn't have taken more than a minute."

"Well, that's too fast for blowfish poison. I'm starting to think we might looking at something based around one of those snake venoms that can knock a bird out of the air in a second or less. Put Freddie back on."

I put Freddie back on.

He went back to work and I went back to feeling helpless. I stood with my fists in my pockets, shifting my weight from my toes to my heels. Freddie was examining the shrunken lemon. *Yeah*, I heard him say, *there's something. Looks like it might be a needle hole.* For no obvious reason I was thinking of the suit I'd been wearing when Bram Shapiro died on me. I didn't think it would clean up and even if it did, I wasn't sure how I'd feel about it. Pity. I hadn't liked it that much when I'd bought it, and now I was going to miss it.

"Hey," Freddie Small said, and he seemed to be including me.

"What?" I said.

"Getting somewhere."

I wish I'd been paying attention to whatever he'd been doing. I can't tell you what worked the trick, but it happened in one miraculous moment. She was gone, and then she was back. She arched up and took a sudden breath, and all her colour returned in a flood. It was as if there had been two of us alone in the room, and now we were three.

"Anything else you need to do?" I said.

"I don't think so," he said. "That's it."

Freddie moved aside, and I moved in and took her hand.

"Hey, Julie," I said. "Feel this?" I squeezed her fingers, and felt them twitch. They were still cold, but they moved.

"You're going to be fine, now," I told her. She screwed up her eyes as if there was sand in them, and she tried to swallow. I remembered how I'd felt when I went through the same stage of recovery, and I went to the bathroom for a wet towel to dampen her lips and tongue. While I was in there, the bedside phone rang. Freddie abandoned the repacking of his tote bag, and took over the rehydration job while I answered.

It was the desk clerk. He'd sounded dubious when Freddie had arrived. He sounded positively testy now.

"Listen," he said. "I know you're a cop and everything, but you and I are gonna have to have words."

"Did my people arrive?"

"If by your people you mean the travelling circus, I've got them right here."

"Don't get into a flap. Just send them up."

"I'm responsible for anything that goes on in this building."

"Send them on up, and we'll be out of the way before the end of your shift."

Five minutes later there was a knock on the door, and I opened it to find the Reverend Henry Zeno with son Michael and three of the women from his congregation, all but one of them neighbors of mine. The exception was Edwina Dodds, Johnny's terrifying sister, who was also a Licensed Practical Nurse at the Riverlands Health Care Center. She didn't live close, but I'd seen her often enough.

Michael was pushing the crummiest-looking wheel-chair you could ever imagine. It was like a junk sculpture. It belonged with the Church's community bus and looked as if it had been salvaged and patched up after a lifetime of hard service in a war zone.

"Lady needs a ride?" the Reverend said.

"Yeah," I said, "come in."

I ushered them all in, and then I checked the silent corridor in both directions before I closed the door.

"She's right through there, on the bed," I told them. "Just give her a couple of minutes while she gets into some clothes."

They moved to the couches to sit, and Michael opened up the big cabinet with the TV in it and turned it on. I went back into the sleeping area, where Freddie was zipping up his tote bag with his gear all packed away. Julie had her face turned away and her arm raised, the back of her hand against her forehead.

"Thanks, Freddie," I said. "Is there a fee?"

"Not this time," he said.

I lowered my voice so that Julie wouldn't hear.

"Has she been asking for her boy?" I said.

"She knows he's gone," Freddie said.

We shook hands, and then he picked up his bag and left. I heard him exchange brief greetings with the Reverend and then I heard the door open and close.

I sat on the bed and said, "How's it going?"

Without lowering her hand or turning her head, she said, "That was the worst thing ever." Her voice sounded scratchy and dry.

"Believe me," I said, "I know. We need to leave. Can you dress yourself?"

"He said I'd better hope it was you that found me. And that I wouldn't get Christopher back until I did what he wanted."

"Did you tell him there was nothing left to give him?"

"First he laughed in my face and then he spat in it. Next thing I know, I'm flat on the floor and he's dragging me across the carpet. He knew all about you coming out to see me. He knew every move we'd made. He isn't human."

"Of course he's human. All it proves is that he's been watching you."

I went back to the others.

"I think she could use some help with dressing," I said, and Edwina Dodds and the other women went through to see to the job.

There was nothing I could do for the moment, so I sat down alongside the Reverend. He said, "Where to, John?"

"Back to my place, I suppose," I said. "See if she'll stay

put this time."

It took them about twenty minutes to have her ready. When I went through she was sitting on the bed fully-dressed, but hanging onto the edge of it. It was as if she was game, but it was all she could do to stay upright. Edwina and her crew had washed her face and they'd combed her hair.

Michael brought the wheelchair and we helped her into it. She protested that she could manage, but Michael and I had to pretend she was doing it while we took an arm each and lifted her across.

First we got the all bags out, then we came back for the patient. I think it was the Community Bus in the parking lot that was annoying the desk clerk most. Michael had managed to leave it standing under the brightest of the spotlights and in the clerk's line of sight through the entrance doors. It was ancient and it had been hand-painted, and it looked as if it had spent many years being regularly stoned and shot at. There was a roof rack for camping trips and a chair hoist on the rear. It looked like the tour bus for a troupe of Albanian acrobats.

When it had gone, I went back inside for a final word with the clerk. He wore a dark blazer with a white shirt and light gray pinstriped trousers. He was so clean-cut and well-groomed, you could have sliced him out of stiff card with a laser.

"When did you start your shift?" I said.

"If you're asking did I check her in," he said, "yes I did."

"But it wasn't you that I first spoke to on the phone."

"Reservation enquiries are handled by our call center."

"What about the man who came and took the boy away? Would you have seen him?"

His manner changed slightly at this. I thought I spotted a sudden uncertainty in his eyes.

"I guess I would," he said.

"What did he look like?"

He made as if to speak. But then he closed his mouth and made a helpless gesture.

"Average?" I prompted.

"I guess. I took him for the father. Didn't look that close."

"If I showed you pictures, could you pick him out?"

"I'm not so sure I could."

"Don't worry about it," I said, and went out to my car.

FIFTEEN

I'D GIVEN them my keys to get into the house, so the lights were on when I got back. Squeezing past the suitcases that had returned to block my hallway, I walked in on a scene that was almost a replica of the one earlier; my TV was playing, most of them were sitting watching it, and Edwina Dodds was in the bedroom with Julie Boudreaux.

A second or two after I arrived, she emerged and said, "That's it, I'm gone. Night, y'all."

"Thanks for this," I said. "I appreciate it."

"She threw up in the van," Edwina said.

"I'm sorry. You want me to clean that up for you?"

"The boys can do it. We put her in your bed and she went straight off to sleep. I put a little gris-gris bag under her pillow. Can't harm, might help."

At the Reverend's word, all the others roused themselves from before the TV and followed him out. I thanked each in turn, and watched from the doorway as they dispersed to their homes on foot and Michael climbed behind the wheel of the bus. It was garaged somewhere else, but I'm not sure where.

When the people were gone from sight and the bus had been driven away, I locked the front door and then double-checked the locks on all the other doors and windows. After that, I levered off my shoes and went into the bedroom where Julie Boudreaux was lying.

What I'd thought looked like candlelight proved to be exactly that. A yellow taper stood by the bedside, fixed to a plate by a few drops of its own wax. I later learned that somewhere in the spectrum of vodoun beliefs, a yellow candle was meant to drive off one's enemies. Alongside the plate was a small array of simple charms.

Would they work? I'd no reason to think so. But I didn't even think of clearing them away.

I watched her for a few moments to be sure that she was still breathing, the way you do for your children when they're very young or your parents when they're getting old. I noted that the sheets had been changed. I'd been intending to do that for days. Her clothes had been folded and placed on a chair nearby.

Her face was turned toward the light. She looked like a different person when she was asleep. There was none of the prickliness, none of the attitude. As I watched, her expression tightened up into a wince; it was a tiny thing, like a ripple across water, and she made a tiny sound to go with it.

I knew all about the nightmares. The candle dipped as I moved closer, and I leaned over to place the gentlest touch of my hand on her shoulder.

"Easy," I whispered, and I felt her subsiding into calm.

When she was quiet again, I backed out of the room and half-closed the door so I'd be able to hear if she called out. I loosened my tie, and then I took out my gun and laid it on the coffee table in front of the couch. I sat down with it just within reach.

What was the best thing to do? With the voodoo cops around, the answer would have been simple. But they weren't, so it wasn't. Julie Boudreaux would co-operate with nobody but me. I was the walking dead man, the one with the mark of the one-man white bizango. For her, I was the voodoo cop now.

I didn't think that Christopher would come to any immediate harm. Legendre was the boy's hero, which I imagined would make him easy to handle. Unless he'd seen anything of what had happened to his mother, in which case the situation could be very different.

Either way, the long-term prospects for his safety were not good. The only effective threat is the one you're actually prepared to carry out. And Eddie Vinson seemed to have few inhibitions on that score.

I switched off the light and stretched out on the couch. I could have used one of the spare beds, but then I wouldn't have been able to hear if she started to panic or move around. I didn't expect to sleep, but I was grateful for the chance to rest.

I'd close my eyes. Just for a while. That was all.

When I eventually die, I only hope that it feels the way you do when you're dog-tired and sleep catches you out for a few moments. It's a feeling like when you dive to the bottom of the pool and touch the tiles only to rise back to the surface again. You lie back and you get that sense of utter bliss as the blood leaves the brain, and then you wake only moments later into the memory of how it felt.

It's happened to me only two or three times in my life, and it's always left me with the perception that I just came out of some wonderful place that I can't quite remember. Sometimes I wonder if that's the reality behind the idea of heaven. That to die is to go there and not return. To that secret garden, that place through the door in the wall.

All I can say is, if that's heaven, then staring at the inside of your own shroud while you wait for the eviscerating knife has got to be something close to hell. It was a dubious privilege to have experienced both.

I woke to find a dark shape looming over me.

For a moment I panicked. My gun was on the table, well within grabbing distance, but the figure stood in the way. Then I realized that it was Julie. She had a hold of my hand, and she was tugging at it. That was what had woken me; not the sound of her rising, not the noise of her moving around.

She was trying to get me to stand. I was so sleep-jumbled that I didn't immediately grasp the idea. The only light in the room was a faint spillage from the street lamps outside, and she was a rim-lit silhouette against it. I couldn't see her face but I could see the fine down on the edge of her skin, ablaze in the backlight like a snapshot of the sun's corona. All that I could see of what she was wearing was the shape of her through the nightdress they'd put her into.

She spoke. "Scared," was all she said, and then she tugged at my hand even harder.

So hard, in fact, that the force of it brought me halfway to my feet, and once I was there she wouldn't let me fall back. Before I could get my balance, she was moving back and drawing me with her. My first stumbling step had me crash into the coffee table. It moved about a foot, and I heard my gun skitter across the surface and pitch onto the carpet. I wanted to stop and retrieve it, but she was still pulling me onward.

I followed her into the bedroom and I feel guilty about it even now. Although I'm not even sure that I should. I'd had exactly the same experience. I understood what it was that she needed in its aftermath. The only difference between us was that for me, no-one had been there.

I know I crawled out at some point during the night, when I retrieved my gun from the floor. The bed seemed huge and I felt as if we were buried deep in the middle of it, and it never even crossed my mind that I shouldn't return. I slid back into the zone of warmth and pulled the covers over. Julie Boudreaux was hot to the touch. The gun went under the pillow, pointing up toward the bedhead with the grip where I could reach it in a hurry, should I need to.

A gris-gris bag to sleep on is all very well. But for real protection, give me ordnance every time.

SIXTEEN

IT WAS the neighbor's cars that woke me, as those who had work set out for it the next morning. I lay there for a while, looking at the slats of light across the ceiling. At first I couldn't face the idea of getting out of bed, but that feeling passed in ten minutes or less and I sneaked out to the shower with as little disturbance as I could manage. She was still asleep when I picked out some clean clothes and took them into the hallway to dress.

After that I went into the kitchen and started to put together a guest breakfast, opening and closing the cupboard doors in silence. A guest breakfast involves all those things you keep in but never have yourself; those rolls from the back of the freezer, that honey from the back of the cupboard, milk in a jug instead of straight out of the carton, juice in real glasses instead of Happy Meal souvenir cups.

Before too long, I heard her moving around. Shortly after that, she came to the breakfast bar. She was wearing a big robe, looking heavy-lidded and, without her makeup, a good few years younger.

I said, "How does it feel?"

"You mean, this head of mine?" she said. "Thick as a bucket of river mud."

I busied myself at the microwave, studying the front like I'd never programmed it before, and then I thought I'd better just plunge right in.

"There's something I want to say," I said.

Exactly the same thing must have been on her mind. "You mean about last night?" she said.

"It wasn't in my mind to take advantage."

"I'm not saying you did. That's not how I usually behave, either. I don't know where it came from. It doesn't feel very . . . "

"Appropriate?"

"No."

"Shall we just leave it?"

"I think we'd best."

Well, we'd sorted that out, but now there was an awkward silence.

I said, "Are you hungry?" but she shook her head.

"Coffee? Tea?"

"Just some hot water," she said.

That would be easy enough. I made some for her, and she sat holding the mug with both hands. The rolls and cereal sat before her, untouched.

"I have a real problem," she said.

"I know."

"I can't give him what he wants. But if I don't, he won't leave me alone. If he could do what he did to us, what might he do to Christopher?"

"What kind of control do you have over the business?"

"Everything," she said. "I'm it. Power of attorney came into effect when Kenny was declared incapable. Legendre knows that. I can't even give him any excuses."

"We think his real name's Eddie Vinson."

"Well," she said, lightening momentarily, "that dents his mystique a little."

I sat down at the table with her and said, "So what does he actually want?"

"He wants me to raise a cash loan against the value of the business, and then hand him the money. Then he says he'll send Christopher back to me and disappear."

"And if you don't?"

"He still disappears. But he takes Christopher with him. Or worse. I don't know."

"You have to play along with him for now," I said.

She looked at me with a bewildered frown.

"How?" she said. "I told you I'm broke. I can't pay him anything."

"Just go through the motions of doing what he asks," I said. "Don't worry, I'll be helping you all along the way."

"He specifically said no police."

"I'm the only cop he's going to see," I said, "and he thinks he's got me broken. We don't have much choice in this. We don't know where he is or how to reach him, and we won't until he contacts us. We've got to let him make a move. He will be in touch. That's the one thing we can be certain of."

SHE RAN a bath, and I had a general self-conscious tidy-around of the house while she was in it. The phone didn't ring all morning. By the time she appeared, I'd put the cereal away and turned the untouched rolls into tuna sandwiches.

She was wearing a gingham cotton blouse and cream linen pedal-pushers. Elegant enough, but ordinary. I don't think she'd done much with her hair other than blow-dry it and push it back behind her ears. She got up onto the barstool where she'd been sitting earlier, put her elbows on the mica top, and made a despondent face. We did have an actual dining table in another room but that was for polishing and looking at, not for eating off.

She said, "I'm sorry I insulted your house. I didn't mean to. It's not so bad here."

"But you're used to better," I said.

"We weren't always rich," she said. "We got married in college. We had a two-roomed apartment and we didn't own our furniture. Then Kenny made a lot of money fast. You forget. You start to think that because you've got it, it must be because you somehow deserve it. You start to think that because you did something right it must mean you can do no wrong."

"How will you get by after this?"

"I'll have to find a job, take some courses, start a business. Whatever it takes." She glanced around. "Maybe move into a place just like this."

"You've already apologized," I said. "You don't have to go overboard."

"I mean it. You've got something worth having, here. When everything hit the fan I didn't even have anyone around me I could tell about it, let alone ask for help. All the people we called friends . . . well, none of that was real friendship, it was just socializing. You only stay afloat in that crowd for as long as your usefulness lasts. A friend in need is an instant leper."

I indicated the food, which she showed no sign of having noticed.

"No appetite?" I said, and she shook her head.

I said, "It's not in his interests to injure your kid."

"I know that," she said. "Christopher worships him. Ever since he showed him how to fix the Nolan boy. He'll give him no trouble. He'll put his head right on the block if he tells him to do it."

THE CALL came just after mid-day, and it came on my cell phone. Julie's own phone was missing, and we found out why; he'd taken it from the hotel suite and he was using the redial on it to contact us now.

He said, "You know who this is?" and the hair on my back tingled.

"You took your time," I said.

"Needed to be sure she'd be awake. Put her on."

"Talk to me first."

"Ah," he said. "The hero. All those protective instincts coming to the fore. How is she?"

"Fine, given the near-death experience you gave her."

"Yeah, and I bet you really reaped the benefit. Death and sex. One hell of a mix, or what?"

"I don't know what you're talking about."

"Yes, you do. Don't thank me. Call it your commission. Are you blushing?"

I think I was. Out of the corner of my eye, I saw her coming into the room. I'd picked up the phone so quickly that I don't think she'd heard it ring, but then she must have overheard me speaking.

I said, "Get to your point."

"Okay. I don't care what she does and I don't care how she does it, but five hundred thousand will make me go away. What's the matter?"

I must have seemed to hesitate.

"Nothing," I said.

"You thought I'd ask for more? I'm a realist. I know what she's worth and I know what she can raise."

Actually, I'd been thinking that it was a lot.

I said, "Say we go along."

"You'd better."

"Tell me how to get it to you."

"First things first. Get the cash. None of those cop tricks like marked bills or radio trackers. Try anything and I'll know."

"And then you'd do what? Kill Christopher? I don't imagine you were thinking of taking an apprentice."

"Now, there's an idea," he said. "But I don't think so."

I was aware that Julie was signaling to me. I knew she'd been watching me and trying to work out the drift of the conversation, but I'd been avoiding meeting her eyes in case she threw my concentration.

"She wants to talk to you," I said.

"Put her on."

I gave her the phone. She put it to her ear and half-turned away from me.

"Legendre," she said, "I'm sorry. I apologize for ever opposing you. Please forgive me. Please look after Christopher while he's in your care."

There was a pause while she listened. I didn't like this part of it. It's always disturbing to see that kind of submissive vulnerability, and that's redoubled when it's someone you know.

After a few moments she said, "Can I speak to him?"

Another pause, and then:

"No, I understand, I apologize for asking." She looked at me and held out the phone. "He wants you again."

I took it from her.

"Yes?"

"Keep that phone charged up and close by. I'll call again when you have the money."

"Why don't we call you?"

"Because the moment this call is done, this phone goes straight in the trash. You think I don't know they can track you with one of these things? As if giving you brain cancer wasn't enough."

"Legendre?" I said. "I think you're full of shit."

"Five hundred thousand buys you the right to your opinion," he said, and hung up.

SEVENTEEN

F OR THE rest of that day and the early part of the next, we played a game. The name of it was, Pretend to Get the Money. We drove to her bank, sat in the foyer for ten minutes, came out empty-handed and went to a coffee shop in the same shopping plaza where we killed about an hour, checking our watches every ten minutes or so.

We were working on the assumption that Vinson would be watching us for at least some part of the process. That wouldn't take any supernatural talent, just routine lowlife invisibility, the kind that allows them to walk away with your briefcase in a crowded railway station or steal the laptop computer out of your car while you're getting a newspaper.

Julie kept looking out for him until I told her not to. We needed him to feel that everything was going his way. For that very reason, I'd resisted the temptation to call him Eddie during the phone call, much as I'd wanted to score something back for that 'sex and death' remark.

That had been a worryingly accurate shot, and an embarrassing one.

But I didn't believe he'd been watching us that closely. I had to remind myself that despite the voodoo front and the pharmaceutical backup he was, by trade and by training, a con artist. Con artists don't need a formal education but they're expert manipulators, the unprincipled street fighters of human psychology.

When the hour was over, we went back to the bank and this time we asked to speak to one of the managers. There followed an odd interview . . . he assumed that Julie wanted to straighten out her financial affairs and that I was some kind of advisor that she'd brought along to help her do it, while I simply wanted a few of those paper bands that they put around the money. In the course of the discussion I learned that the Boudreauxs had a little under fifteen thousand dollars in a personal checking account but that the business account was showing a deficit of more than three times that amount.

Because of the size of the debt he kept trying to get us back onto the subject, which meant that rather than straightening out Julie's affairs I had to straighten out the manager. I don't recall what he said that set me off, but I do remember Julie hauling on my arm to pull me back while I leaned over his desk with my shirt open, pointing to my scar and asking if he thought it meant that I wasn't a man of serious purpose.

Five minutes later we were walking out with everything we'd asked for, which included a package that looked as if it might have contained half a mil in currency but which actually contained thirty back issues of USA TODAY from the staff coffee lounge. Julie carried it out to the car, and I covered her with my hand inside my coat and my eyes all over the parking lot like I was guarding Ghandi from a second pop.

In the car and driving away, she said, "Thanks."

"Nothing to it," I said.

"I haven't had anybody stand up for me in months."

The sky was hazy and the day was humid, and the air conditioning was struggling to cope so that the car was smelling like a cold wet field. We were less than five minutes away from the bank when my phone started to ring.

There was nowhere to pull over and so I took it out of my pocket and handed it to her, still ringing.

"What if it's him?" she said.

"I'm expecting it will be," I said. "Press any button other than the red one."

She put it to her ear.

"Yes, Legendre," she said.

I must have made a noise, because she shot me a look.

I could tell he was doing a lot of talking, because she was doing a lot of listening. I was thinking that the timing of the call was confirmation that he'd been watching us, and I wondered if he was watching us now. How would I know? I couldn't even remember the face that I was looking for. Julie had tried to describe him for me, but all I'd learned was that his face was kind of ordinary and his hair was kind of brown and that he looked a little bit like that actor in *Star Trek* who hadn't been in it for very long and whose name she couldn't remember.

I looked in my mirror, saw there was a white Mitsubishi pickup behind us, and recalled that he'd been with us all the way from the plaza.

Julie was saying, "Wait a minute, I've got to write this down." And then her tone sharpened as she said, "Never mind 'just listen', I'm not going to risk my son's life for the sake of some detail I missed." She was looking in the glove box, so I nudged her shoulder and then pointed her to the notepad and pen that I kept tucked into the sun visor.

She listened, scribbled, and I gave as much of my attention as I dared to the pickup truck in my mirror. I was trying to make out whether the driver had a phone to his ear, but he was keeping just enough of a distance for me not to be able to say. I touched my brakes, he drew a little closer.

It wasn't him. Not unless he was in the guise of a large woman in a tractor cap. The pickup made a turnoff onto one of the farm roads and I heard Julie saying, "Okay, I'll tell him."

"Tell me what?" I said when she'd ended the call.

"You have to stay in the house while I deliver the money. If he calls and you're not there, it's all off."

"Did he say when?"

"Tonight. I've got to pick up a Nike sports bag and put the money in that. I'll get a text message on this phone with the name and location of a supermarket. I have to be at the employee door five minutes before the shift changes over. Someone will have fixed the door so it's open. I'm to leave the money in a numbered staff locker in the corridor and then let the door close behind me as I go out."

"That's it?"

"That's it. What's it all about?"

"Did he specifically say a Nike sports bag?"

"Yeah, a blue one."

"Here's what I bet will happen. How many people do you get in one supermarket shift? Within a couple of minutes of the drop, you'll have about thirty or forty of them heading out into the parking lot. At least one of those people will be in the habit of carrying a blue bag just like the one you'll have bought. Eddie or his latest voodoo stooge will be heading off in some other direction with the money switched into something completely different."

"That's devious," she said.

"We need to let him think so," I said.

We stopped at the Wal-Mart on West Main Pine to see if we could pick up the right kind of bag. While Julie was searching the aisles, I realized that she still had my cellular and so I grabbed a senior-citizen shelf-stacker and told him I needed a phone in a hurry. He tried to point me to the pay phones outside the store, but I showed my ID and got the use of a line from the manager's office.

This office was a raised, glass-sided cubicle with a view over the entire sales floor; I could see her moving from the sports section to the checkout, and I timed it so that I was all finished and joining her as she went out of the doors.

Back at the house, we used the kitchen counter as a work space on which to refold the newspapers and pack them into the blue bag. When that was all done, I put a spot of clear glue onto the zipper teeth behind the toggle. It would be enough to frustrate a cursory check, and there wouldn't be the time for anything more.

"So what does this actually do for us?" she said. "Or should I imagine that he won't notice I've paid him off in old newspapers?"

"No," I said, "Don't worry about that. I've got a plan."

"Any chance of letting me in on it?"

"You've got to trust me," I said. "It may not always look like it, but I believe I know what I'm doing."

"You *believe?*"

"My faith against his. He thinks he knows what he's doing, too. But only one of us can be right."

EIGHTEEN

I KNOW IT'S what they always say, but the waiting really was the hardest part. She took the money bag and my phone and went off in my car at eight-thirty. I'd tried to think of ways around it, but in the end I had to stay in the house. Even if he didn't call, he might have someone watching the place and reporting back to him. Along with the rich people he soaked for money, he'd got little people terrorized as well. Useless for tribute, but good for his dirty work. Maurice French had been scared enough to kill for him, and scared enough to die rather than face him when it didn't work out.

You didn't have to shamble or stare to be a 'zombi', I'd come to realize. That only happened in the movies. In life it was a simple matter of being broken to the will of another.

I paced from room to room. I made coffee that I didn't drink. I turned on the TV and then turned it off again. I stretched out on the bed. I got up two seconds later.

Shortly after nine-thirty, there was a faint tap at my kitchen door. If I'd left the TV on I might never have heard it. I switched off the kitchen lights before I went to see who it was. It was dark out there in the yard, and I could just make out the shape of Michael Zeno.

"They got him," he said in a low whisper. "Daddy's working on him now."

"I can't go yet," I said. "He didn't call."

And right at that moment, the house phone rang.

Without putting on the lights, I snatched up the kitchen extension and said, "Lafcadio. Yes? Hello?" but the person at the other end hung up without speaking. I pressed the star button and then six-nine, just in case, but I got a withheld caller ID.

Much as I'd expected. I picked up my coat and rejoined Michael.

"Okay," I said, "we're set. Who did they grab?"

"Just a messenger boy, by the looks of him," Michael said.

I locked the house behind me and then we went across the lawn in a crouch, ducking through a newly-made hole in my fence behind the garage. We yard-hopped all the way to the end of the street and then made a dash for the church, where the security floodlight had been switched off so that we could cross the rough ground beside it without drawing attention.

The church is the oldest building on the street, and also the ugliest. It looks like a big wooden barn. It's sturdy enough, although you'd think it was about to fall down. There's a hand-lettered sign on a board by the door and, up on the roof, a plywood belfry which has never had a bell in it. The boards are so old that they've all turned silver.

Catholicism once tried to absorb voodoo. Instead, vodoun absorbed Catholicism and churches like this one were the result, with its black saints and bizarre symbols and its one-to-one identification of the spirits of the lwa with the spirits of the Lord. Right now the church was in near-darkness, lit mostly by candles down at the far end, with some tinny music playing from an unseen source. There was a small group of people in the circle of light, and I followed Michael Zeno down the center aisle to join them.

My boss was there, and Jimmie Noone and a couple of the others, and two Special Agents from the local FBI office who were standing with their hands in their pockets and looking seriously uneasy, as if they could see their long-term career prospects vanishing if the details of this evening should ever get any wider circulation. On a hard wooden chair at the focus of the group sat a black youth of around fifteen or sixteen years, weeping and hiccuping for breath while the Reverend hugged him and stroked his head.

"Hey, now," the Reverend was saying. "That's the end of it," while the poor kid just sniveled and sniveled.

I sidled up behind Bob Lambert and murmured, "Any problem?"

Without taking his eyes off the boy, Lambert gave a small shake of his head. He said, "Sent a man to follow her, had him stay behind to watch the locker. Boy works in the supermarket. Soon as we knew for sure that he was the one picking up the bag, we grabbed him and brought him out by a side door."

I glanced down at the floor. The blue bag was there, halfway out of a bigger, even cheaper-looking holdall.

Moving over to stand behind the Reverend, I said, "Can he talk to us now?"

The Reverend glanced over his shoulder at me, then turned to the boy and said, "Talk to them, son. God's given you the power to free your mother's soul, it's the least you can do for Him."

It took a while. There wasn't much time, but impatience wouldn't help. Between sniffs and sobs, the boy explained his instructions. He wasn't to look inside the bag, on pain of his momma's death. She'd once asked Legendre for a service and now he held her soul in a bottle. He was to take the bag to the end-of-the-line stop on Jefferson Avenue and be on the ten o'clock trolleybus when it started on its return to the middle of town. He had to get there early enough to be in a specific seat, and then get off two stops later leaving the bag underneath it. That was all.

"I forgot to bring a knife," I said. "Anybody?"

Nobody moved for a moment and then one of the FBI agents said, "Here," and produced a clasp knife, which he opened up and handed to me. I dropped to one knee, and slashed the Nike bag open alongside the full length of the zipper. I took out the newspaper and threw in some of the bank's bill wrappers, torn and crumpled for effect, and then by way of an afterthought I added a brand-new twenty which I made look as if its edge had been caught in one of the seams.

"Time?" I said.

"Nine fifty-four," the other FBI agent said. "Shall I see if we can hold up the bus?"

"No," I said, closing up the holdall, "we need to make it."

"I'm all ready," a voice behind me said, and I turned around to see Michael Zeno rummaging around to rearrange his collar inside the hooded sweatshirt that he was now wearing. It was the messenger kid's.

"Hey, Michael," I said. "Now wait a minute."

"Look at the shape he's in," Michael said, gesturing toward the boy on the chair. "You can't send him out to do this. So who else here looks the part? Let's do the job right."

I looked at the Reverend, but the Reverend simply said, "We discussed this before you got here. He wants to do it."

I had to admit that from a distance, it would be a reasonable deception.

"Nine fifty-six," the FBI agent reported.

What could I do?

"Let's go," I said.

WE DROVE Michael to within one block of Jefferson Avenue, and dropped him to cover the rest of the distance on foot. He ran, and just made it. The bus was standing empty, lights on, doors open, engine running while the driver watched the clock. They'd loaned me a set of FBI binoculars with night vision assistance, and I watched through the tinted windows of their undercover van as Michael paid his fare and moved down the bus to the designated seat.

"Ah, look at that," one of the agents said. "You can see there's no weight in the bag."

"The kid's a car mechanic, not a mime," I said.

It looked as if he was going to be the only passenger, but then a couple of teenaged girls arrived at a run just as the doors were closing. There was the usual gasp and hiss as the driver flipped them open again, and the bus set off a minute late.

We followed at a distance. The grim housing at this end of Jefferson Avenue soon gave way to the garish neon of fast-food signs and budget motels. Michael sat with his hand up to his head and his face turned away from the window.

The first stop was right by a gas station, and no-one was waiting. The bus slowed and then sailed on past it. The road widened to six lanes after that and we got held back at some lights, but we caught up again a couple of minutes later. The bus was pulling away from the second stop, and Michael had disembarked. He was walking off into the darkness with the hood on the sweatshirt pulled up over his head. Above him, and out of the shadows, rose an entire artificial hillside floodlit for night-time crazy golf.

I hadn't realized how much I'd been holding my breath until then. We stayed with the bus, and our FBI driver risked getting us alongside at the next lights so that I could take a closer look at the new people who'd boarded.

"Anyone there look familiar?" one of the agents said.

"Not to me," I said.

I'd have brought Julie along, if only she'd got back to the house in time. Alone among us, she could pick out Eddie Vinson from a crowd. As it was, my best hope had to be that the sight of him might trigger a memory. But we followed the bus the entire length of its route, and I didn't recognize anyone. Nobody even seemed likely.

The deal was that, unless I was certain, no-one was to go storming in.

So no-one went storming in.

As the bus reached the end of its run, one of the FBI men called ahead to get it taken out of service. We met it at the bus garage. The driver stood by his vehicle, nervously trying to work out what he might have done wrong. One of the agents stopped to talk to him and the other one came on board with me. By now I'd become convinced that something had scared him off, and he hadn't even been near.

We walked the whole length of the bus. There was no bag under the designated seat, or under any of the others.

WHEN I got back, my car was on the street and Julie was inside the house.

"Where did you go?" she said. "He told you to stay here."

"I did," I said. "I stayed and took his call."

"Then where did you go?"

I started to explain, but I was interrupted by a tapping at the kitchen door. She followed me through as I went to open it and let in both of the FBI men. One of them appeared to have slipped and fallen in the darkness of my yard.

"What's this shit I got all over me?" he said, seeing himself in the light for the first time.

"Cooking oil," I said.

"It's black!"

"It's burned. You'll find some old rags in the cupboard."

He was dabbing at himself and making some unhappy noises as I drew Julie away into another part of the house.

"Who are they?" she said.

"Federal agents," I told her, and at that moment the unsoiled one squeezed past us with a polite nod.

"Miz Boudreaux," he said pleasantly, and then she watched as he opened up my hallway cupboard and changed the DAT tape on the recording device that had been linked into the house phone line.

The other one called me for something else then, and when I returned Julie was nowhere to be seen. I found her in the bedroom, curled up in the dark with a pillow over her head. She was shaking uncontrollably.

I sat on the bed beside her and said, quietly, "If it's worked the way I meant it to, he now thinks we paid over the money and some small-time thief on the bus has got lucky and ripped it off. His problem is that it happened on his side of the net, not ours. What's he going to do? He can't clean you out twice."

She threw the pillow off and looked at me through tousled hair. "And when did the FBI come into it?" she said, lifting herself up on one elbow and blowing some of the wisps aside.

"My boss brought them in. And I called him while Freddie Small was working on you at the hotel."

"And that's it?"

"That's all of it."

"It's a stupid plan," she exploded. "Some small-time thief on the bus got lucky? Jesus Christ. You think he's going to swallow that? He's a Vodoun master, not a moron. If I'd known that was the great design, I'd have said forget it right there and then."

"Exactly my reason for keeping it from you."

"You bastard," she said. "If my son suffers after what you did tonight, I'll get a knife and finish what they started on you. Get away from me. Get right away. I don't ever want to see you." She slammed down onto the mattress and planted the pillow back over her head.

"I live here," I pointed out.

"I don't care," she shouted from under the pillow.

His next call came just a few minutes before midnight.

NINETEEN

IT WAS the house phone. I didn't wait for him to identify himself, but jumped straight in. "Well, congratulations," I said. "You're half a mil richer. So where is he?"

"Not so fast, blue boy," he said. "That was the first stage."

"First stage my ass," I said angrily, "what are you trying to pull? This is a done deal and we've completed our end of it. If this isn't going to be a conversation about getting the boy back, don't even talk to me."

And with that I slammed the phone down.

I hadn't planned it that way. It just felt right. One hundred per cent confidence that our end of the bargain had been met. One hundred per cent annoyed when he didn't meet his. The slightest hesitation or failure of nerve, and he'd know we were dealing him bullshit.

I could see that the local FBI men, listening over on the other side of the room via their plug-in earpieces, had both gone pale.

After a few moments, the phone started to ring again. I didn't pick it up right away. I was aware of movement and glanced up to see Julie in the doorway. Her eyes met mine as I reached for the phone. She looked wary. But she didn't look away.

This time, it was him launching in without giving me the chance to speak.

"Let's get one thing straight," he said. "You don't ever interrupt me or hang up on me. You even irritate me mildly and I'll cut this boy's throat and hold the phone where you can hear it squirt. I am *that* far away from it.

Do you understand me, zombi?"

"What did you call me?"

"Asshole on a fucking stick is what I call you. I want to make sure you understand me, so listen like you've at least some chance of grasping it. I . . . need . . . more."

"You got half a mil," I said. "The tit's dry."

"That's not my problem, I've had some unexpected expenses."

I breathed an expletive and gave it a moment so that he could imagine hearing my heart sink.

Then I said, "How much?"

"Another hundred thou."

"From where?" I demanded. "You know exactly what her position is. So you know you've cleaned her out."

"This comes out of you," he said. "And if you're going to start to whine about it, the price is gonna go up."

"If that's what you're thinking, you'd better kill the boy right now and save yourself some McDonalds money," I said.

The FBI men were all but covering their heads. Moving slowly and in complete silence, Julie drew out a chair and settled opposite me. Her eyes stayed on me and her expression never changed.

On the other end of the line, Eddie Vinson said, "What are you talking about? What kind of a remark is that?"

"You can run the price up all you like," I said. "I don't have it and I can't get it. If you've been watching my house then you've seen the realtor's sign. I've got a soon-to-be ex-wife whose attorney has frozen our savings and attached two-thirds of my salary. I don't have an asset to my name until this place is sold, and I'll consider myself lucky if I get to hold onto a fraction of that."

There was a silence.

Then the Great Legendre said, "Well, how much can

you manage?"

And it was then that I knew I had him.

TWENTY

THE NEXT day was the Friday. I'd already had to call and put the girls off for the weekend. He'd wanted to set up a meeting for that morning until I'd pointed out to him that I'd need the day for all the running-around first. I'd bargained him down to thirty-five thousand. I told him that it would have to come out of some assets that my soon-to-be-ex didn't know about. The haggling wasn't really necessary, but it gave the whole setup an edge of credibility.

I think the thing of it was, he'd let slip two fortunes already. To lose a third on a bus might be a sickener, but it wasn't without precedent. I could imagine him staring into the slashed-up bag and thinking, What is it with me? And then lowering his head and then taking a breath, before wearily stirring himself to begin it all over.

That afternoon, after the banks had closed, I followed the crowds down to the farmer's market in the Old Town. To be honest, a lot of it isn't all that old. But then the really old parts of town smell of pee and decay, and their nightlife is the kind you trap or scratch. This area is a few squares and blocks next to Jefferson Park that have been rehabilitated for shopping and leisure. Which means that by day you can buy a T-shirt and in the evening you can drink beer and listen to tourist jazz.

Right by the market is a paved square with an antique fountain and a beignet stand. The beignet stand is an open-air café with a canvas awning and a flimsy waist-high barrier to contain the seating area. Tables are crowded in around a central island where they froth the coffee and fry the fancy donuts.

I circled it a few times until I saw a table coming free, and then I dodged through the barrier and claimed it before it had even been cleared and wiped. The bag that I was carrying went under my seat. I kept my foot on the strap, so no-one would be able to sneak it away when I wasn't looking. It contained, not newspaper this time, but wads of dead bills provided by the FBI. They looked real, because they were. But they'd been taken out of circulation and treated with something that would turn them yellow within a few hours of exposure to light.

The table was cleared and then the waitress came. She wore a crisp white blouse, with braces on her teeth and a stud in the side of her nose.

I said, "Can I just get coffee?" and she said, "Sure," and moved away.

And then for a while I sat there, drumming my fingers and wondering how long I'd have to wait. I was aware of a group of nearby tourists giving me foul looks for grabbing the table they'd had their eye on, but they passed on by. I took in the scene. Smell of frying dough, early weekend crowd, busy square, busy streets. Tower Records had its doors open and was providing the soundtrack.

Then I scanned the other patrons. No-one met my eyes or paid me any attention. My coffee came. I picked the creases out of the edge of the tablecloth. It was white linen under a sheet of glass, the whole arrangement anchored with drawing-board clips. I neatened up the clips.

Nothing continued to happen.

Someone came by with a jug and freshened my coffee without asking. I heard a clattering sound and looked across to see two mounted park security officers riding through on the far side of the fountain, the shoes of their horses striking the paving like flints. There was a flash as one of the kids sitting on the edge of the fountain took a picture.

A voice said, "Excuse me?"

I looked up and saw a young man standing there. He had gelled blond hair and he was wearing a big, loose, short-sleeved shirt. There was a magazine in one hand, a latte in the other. Behind him, my grumpy tourist group had moved in and were getting settled.

He said, "I couldn't keep on hogging the table all to myself. May I share yours for a minute?"

I glanced around. This was not a welcome development.

"I'm waiting for someone," I said.

He half-hesitated and glanced about him as if momentarily unconvinced that we were occupying the same planet; giving me the benefit of the doubt in a mental *can-such-assholes-be?* debate.

"Until they get here?" he said, in a tone that was appealing to me to agree and keep it nice.

If I didn't want to become a center of attention, then I didn't seem to have much choice.

"Why not?" I said.

He pulled out a chair and sat down. The tables weren't that big, and everybody was crammed in so close that he had to squeeze. At twenty-five or less, he wasn't a candidate and he didn't fit the pattern of Legendre's messengers so far. But he was a complication.

"Is anything wrong?" he said.

"Not a thing," I said, and made an effort to turn my attention outward again.

But my attitude had made him uncomfortable, and he said, "Look, if my being here really bothers you, I'll move."

"Please don't," I said, thinking *Please do*, but resigning

myself to being stuck with him for a minute or two and not wanting to do anything that would make a scene or extend the time. We settled into an uneasy co-existence, him turning to his magazine and me looking out into the square, strangers in our separate spaces. Body language alone ought to make it obvious there was no subterfuge here.

I could hear sirens. Ours. I tensed, but they were several streets away and not heading in this direction. Two cars at least, though. An obvious police presence was the last thing I needed right now.

Without raising his eyes from his magazine, the young man said, "Somebody called the sports arena and claimed to have planted a bomb under one of the stands. It's a hoax, of course. But they'll have to evacuate and search the place to be a hundred per cent sure. Which means all the street policing around here is going to be stretched a little thin for a while."

He looked up at me then, met my eyes, and laid down the magazine.

I reached for that moment of recognition I'd been waiting for, the one that would restore my certainties and make everything fall into place. But none came. He didn't even look anything like the figure I'd imagined. In my head he'd been . . . I don't know, he'd been lots of people. None of them like this. None so young, none so ordinary.

He said, "So where is it?"

"Under the table," I said.

"Push it over to me."

I shoved the bag with my foot. He reached down and drew it up into his lap.

"Jesus Christ," he said, looking down. "I told you put it in something inconspicuous. Who or what the hell is Cradle of Filth?"

It was the band logo on the music bag that I'd taken from Melissa's room. "I had to improvise," I said. "Look around. All the kids are carrying them."

"Yeah, and me without my skateboard. I hope you're not trying to pull anything after all we discussed."

"Just doing what I'm told," I said. "Since apparently I'm your zombi now."

He grinned. And although I'd failed to recognize him, not even by his voice, I had no problem in believing.

"You're starting to understand," he said.

His guard was dropped for a moment as he worked at the bag to get it unzipped. Despite his air of confidence, I knew he was desperate. Everyone he'd sent had let him down, so now he was risking himself. He must have been here well ahead of me, watching out for any hint of a trap, only committing himself when he was sure.

"So where's Christopher?" I said.

"I'll send him to you when I'm satisfied."

"What reassurance do I have?"

"Fuck you, and that's all you get."

I sensed one or two heads turn, and so did he. He went quiet for a moment. He'd got the bag open now, and he was looking inside. The money couldn't be faulted. There was no way of telling that they'd be gag bills by this time tomorrow.

He stuck his arm in, right down to the bottom of the bag like a kid rummaging for the best deal in the bran tub. Feeling around inside for any bugs or tracking devices, he said, "Believe it or not, I know exactly what you went through. My teacher did it to me. Or for me, however you want to look at it. The difference between me and you is that some of us have the character to come out of it stronger."

He glanced up at me again, and without any warning

he blew a quick puff of air into my face. I flinched, and felt my chair move. I'd probably reacted far more than a normal person would.

He was grinning again.

"Maybe I should take you with me," he said. "My zombi to do my bidding. I could send you out to do my shitwork, jobs like this."

Half the daylight seemed to be blotted out as the horses and riders from the park security patrol passed right by the stand. Eddie Vinson loosely closed the music bag and sat back in a motion that was just a shade too fast not to look guilty.

He didn't strike me as a powerful figure right then. I saw him for what he was. A one-time reform school kid with a knack for the hustle, now just another con clamming up when a uniform went by. He was looking the other way, holding the bag shut, waiting for it all to be over. I could hear the horses coming to a stop by the rail a few yards behind me. Some of the tourists were snapping pictures of them, one or two of them standing up to do it.

And from behind my back, I could hear one of the park security riders calling down to one of the other tables and saying, "Hey, Major. How's it going?"

Vinson's head came up. He looked at me, and then past me. I couldn't help it, I looked over my shoulder.

My boss was sitting three tables away from us. He was looking up at the rider and I saw him give a brief shake of the head and a warning flick of the eyes. I saw it, the rider saw it, and unfortunately Eddie Vinson saw it too.

As I started to turn back to him I found my eye line filled by a fist with a gun in it, my gun, the one he'd taken from my hand underneath the garbage truck under the shopping mall. Before I could do anything about it, he fired.

Bob Lambert was flung back into the table behind him. There were screams. Suddenly everybody in the place was scrambling to be somewhere else. The horses were being wheeled around and I was rising to my feet; as I faced Eddie Vinson I saw him swing the gun around to point it at my chest, right at the center of mass from a distance of two feet or less.

He could think fast, I'll give him that. In that split-second it must have crossed his mind that I might be wearing a protective vest. So to be a hundred per cent certain, he raised the barrel and shot me in the head.

TWENTY ONE

I HEARD THE blast and I felt the kick of the bullet like a punch in the face. I was travelling backwards and down, down, down. I hit the floor, and the floor felt good. Like exactly the kind of place I ought to stay.

There was another gunshot, but I felt nothing. I'd later learn that he'd shot one of the horses. Not fatally, but enough to add to the panic and to take the mounted men out of it.

It was hard to imagine how it could have gone any more wrong.

Well, I suppose he could have gone with his first instinct and shot me in the chest. He'd have killed me then, for sure, because I wasn't wearing a vest at all. Even the lightest of them has enough bulk to be visible.

That decision and his inexperience were what saved me. The gun kicked so hard with the first discharge that on the second, he flinched in anticipation as he fired. The shot went high and the bullet ripped up my scalp. But all he knew was that he'd shot me, and I went down.

Someone was tending to me, some brave soul, and I heard them say, *Oh, God, look at him, he's a goner.* And that galvanized me because I'd heard something so like it before.

"Not yet, I'm not," I managed to say, and I grabbed an arm I couldn't see and used it to haul myself upright. With my free hand I reached around blindly until I caught hold of something that felt like a tablecloth, and which when I yanked hard on it brought stuff crashing onto the ground close by. I tried to use it to wipe at my eyes, but there was too much mess and it didn't work.

"Can somebody get me some water?" I called out to anybody who might be close enough to hear, and I heard a lame voice say, "There are no waiters . . . "

So I tried again with the tablecloth, and this time I managed to clear one sticky eye enough to grope my way to an abandoned carafe on a table that hadn't been knocked over. I emptied it onto my upturned face and felt the ice cubes bounce off my forehead. Another wipe, and I could see again.

The square was partly cleared, partly in chaos. Everybody had scattered from the open spaces and people were now crouching or lying flat behind anything that might be called cover. The wounded horse was down on its side and kicking, its rider still pinned in the saddle, a couple of people trying to get near to pull him free.

Here at the beignet stand, most of the chairs had been upended and the tables shunted around. The free-standing barriers had been shoved aside or knocked over. The only living souls left here were me and the downed Bob Lambert and the four or five unlikely-looking civilian heroes who'd stayed with us. I looked at the tablecloth in my hand and saw that half of it was white and the other half a vivid red, as if it had been dipped in animal blood at the end of a bull run.

I went over to Bob Lambert. A sandy-haired woman was crouching beside him, holding his hand and talking to him. He was flat on his back and moaning, squirming as if it hurt most where his back touched the ground. From what I could see, he'd been struck in the neck. He was bleeding a lot but it wasn't a spraying or a pulsing bleed, the kind you'd get from a severed artery.

I wadded up the cloth in my hands and gave it to the woman to press over the wound, and at that moment a helicopter passed low over the square. It battered us with its downdraft and deafened us with its noise, stirring up a whirlwind in all the litter around us. Bob had his hand on his upper chest with his fingers outspread, as if to press out a delicate belch. I couldn't hear if he was making any sound but his lips were forming the words *Oh, fuck, oh fuck . . .*

"You're gonna be fine," I shouted over the rotor noise, knowing that he probably wouldn't be able to hear me. "Don't worry, I'm onto it . . . "

I was wearing no gun, as per my instructions from the Mighty Goombah, but now I flipped Bob's jacket aside and took his from its belt holster. His preference was a 9mm automatic. I rose to my feet with the unfamiliar weight of it in my hand, and then I turned to the small band of frightened faces and said, "Which way did he go?"

They just stared at me.

"Look, see," I said, "I'm a cop, which way did he go?"

I was struggling to pull out my badge and failing, mainly just managing to drag my pocket inside out. It was embarrassing. I was like some aggressive drunk with my vision blurred and my movements uncoordinated. Either that or they were just too plain shellshocked to respond.

No matter. I looked up. The copter clued me in. It was right there in the sky beyond the farmer's market, circling and turning, marking the trail of its prey like a vulture over a wounded buffalo.

Which I in no small measure resembled myself. I set out across the square, stiff-legged and giddy, walking with only a remote sense of contact with the ground. God alone knows what I must have looked like.

Needless to say, none of this had been part of the plan.

The idea had been for me to make the handover and then step out of the picture while a combined police and

FBI operation swung into play. It had to be the two agencies working together, because the Iberville FBI didn't have the manpower and we didn't have their hardware. I was miked and we had someone watching through binoculars from the top-floor offices over Tower Records, in radio communication with ground surveillance teams on all sides of the square. Bob was close to me in case any intervention was required.

Once the money had changed hands, the plan was for the ground teams to shadow Vinson back to Christopher, switching the pursuit around between them so they wouldn't be spotted. Should they lose him, there was a passive transponder in the lining of the bag that gave out no signal but showed up when one was bounced off it. A search wouldn't reveal anything; the transponder was stitched into the band logo.

It was a tight scheme. When we were setting it up I got the impression that at least half of Iberville law enforcement were to be involved.

A pity that hadn't included the park rangers.

As I went through the market, people were just starting to poke their heads out of their hiding places and quite a few of them dived back again at the sight of me. The market is one long covered building with open sides, basically just a roof on legs. There was fruit and farm produce up at this end giving way to trinkets and hippie clothing the further down you went. Because of the open sides there were a hundred ways in and out of it, and he could have taken any one of them.

My energy was dwindling fast. Had I known how much blood I'd lost, I'd have lain down quietly right there on the concrete. But I got a boost when I realized that I was, quite literally, still on his trail. It was a paper chase. The unzipped bag had been shedding its doctored notes as he ran. They were scattered all down the central aisle of the market. It was a measure of the terror he'd caused that no-one had yet darted out to try helping themselves.

He surely couldn't get far. The entire area was seeded with cops. The only way through them would be to fly or turn invisible, and somehow I didn't think that was going to happen. He wasn't that much a master of the dark arts, just manipulative slime with a few cute poisons and his bag of tricks getting near to exhaustion.

I mis-stepped and lurched into one of the market stalls then, starting a small fruit landslide and getting a sharp reminder that maybe I wasn't as much in control as I thought I was. Someone scuttled out from under the stall, crouching with his backside close to the ground and his hands in the air, and I stopped for a moment in wonder, amazed that anyone could move so fast in such a position.

Then I righted myself, and stalked on.

These were the cheaper stalls now. Wallets for a dollar, new and used junk. Too far away from the heart of the action, scraping along on the occasional sale, half of the stallholders with no more than a dozen words of English. Right at the end, the market petered out. There were a few last empty stands and then an open paved area where trucks unloaded and turned around. This part was for the traders, not the public. It was where the produce sheds were, and dumpsters for the empty boxes and rotted goods. The paved area was like a bullring with gutters for the daily hosing-down. There was only one way out, and a wall of armed police officers was blocking it.

All the weaponry was out and leveled. With the helicopter circling overhead it looked like something out of The Blues Brothers.

Eddie Vinson was at the focus of all the firepower and the only two things keeping the situation alive were his grip on the live hostage that he'd taken, and the gun that he was holding to that officer's head. He was using the man to shield himself, moving to keep him off-balance, roaring something unintelligible and reinforcing his points by ramming the barrel of the handgun—my handgun, still—into the soft spot right under his victim's ear.

I didn't even break my pace. I think if I had, I'd have lost all momentum and crumpled there and then. But I'd been following Eddie and now I'd found him.

I could hear some of the officers calling me to stop or get back as I crossed before them, but it didn't occur to me to comply. Eddie sensed someone approaching on his blind side and quickly turned, dragging his human shield around to keep a live body between us, as if the threat to him had suddenly narrowed to a single point from a specific direction. It would have been a great moment for a marksman shot but unfortunately there wasn't a marksman among them, just street cops with handguns and a couple of pump-action shotguns from the cars.

"No closer!" I could hear Eddie shouting. "I swear to you I'll blow his head right open," and he shoved in the barrel so hard that his hostage yelled out in pain. His hostage was a big blond germanic-looking traffic patrolman; his hostage, I registered with a mental burst of the Alleluia Chorus, was none other than the elusive Dave 'pork-and-run' Corrigan.

If I hadn't lost so much blood I might have taken it all a little more seriously. But I was lightheaded and in the loosest touch with reality now.

Eddie quickly got over his disappointment at seeing me still alive and fixed on me as the one face here that he recognized. "Tell them I want a car," he was shouting, "and I don't want see anyone or anything following me from the air. You'd better be listening to me, Lafcadio. I own your soul, you fucker. You do what I say. Do it, do it now."

I didn't answer him. I called out to his hostage instead.

"Hey, Dave," I said, "how fast can you go down?"

And then without waiting for a reply I swung up Bob Lambert's automatic and fired in a single movement, no taking aim, no chance of warning, no time for this one-man white bizango to react.

Dave Corrigan didn't get the chance to duck, either, and by the time he flinched even that was too late. My shot blinded Eddie Vinson in one eye. But the same bullet also saved him from painful surgery and a lifetime of self-pity by going on to pulp his brain and blow it right out of the back of his skull. The rear of his head flew open like flap doors on the ghost train, and his cerebellum went paintball up the roller door of the produce shed behind him.

Both of them were still standing. Dave Corrigan was so clenched that he was holding the two of them up. But then Vinson kind of melted from around him and slumped to the floor, half-pulling him down before losing his dead man's grip and hitting the ground alone. Some of the others were running forward by then. One of them kicked the handgun away from Vinson and the others caught Dave Corrigan as his legs finally gave way.

Me, I slowly crouched down and laid my borrowed weapon on the ground before me, to be bagged and taken away for the mandatory firearms investigation. Once I was down there, I seemed to lack the strength to get back up again.

I looked across the paving and saw Eddie Vinson staring back at me with his one intact eye. His head didn't look too bad from this side, although I thought I could see daylight through the empty socket.

"You?" I said. "Own my soul?" I said. "I think not."

And then I keeled right over.

TWENTY TWO

THERE WAS still the problem of Christopher. I was out
of it by then so I played no part in what happened,
but they went through Vinson's pockets and found a set of
keys and a parking voucher with a validation stamp from
one of the stores in a nearby building. They located the
car on one of the parking levels and checked it, but it was
empty apart from the rental agreement in the glove box.
The rental was charged to an Amex card in the name of
Norma Lousteau.

So then it was everybody over to the big house in the
garden district, where Norma Lousteau silently,
defeatedly led them upstairs and showed them how to
hook down a trapdoor from which a telescoping metal
ladder then slid. Christopher was up in the attic on a
plastic-covered mattress. He was unmarked but unconscious, and lying in his own waste. He proved to be in a
drugged sleep that it would take him thirty-six hours to
recover from in full. He hadn't eaten in some time, and
was badly dehydrated. Norma Lousteau was placed under
arrest and the SPCA was called to deal with her cats. It
was only at this that she showed any emotion.

Because of Christopher's condition, and with him
being in another hospital, it was almost a week before
Julie Boudreaux came to see me. By then I was sitting up
and the headaches were at least partly under control.
Nobody was prepared to say so but I suspect they were
giving me morphine for those first couple of days. One
can begin to comprehend its appeal. When they switched
me to normal painkillers it was back to reality with an

unpleasantly rough landing.

She sat on the visitor chair by my bed, and asked me how I was feeling.

"Okay when I'm not moving," I said. "I can't get to a mirror. Tell me what I look like, and remember to be kind."

"You're not so bad," she said. "Your face isn't marked, and it's just a little puffy. But all that dressing around your head makes you look like some kind of a swami."

"Well, there you go," I said. "I can be your next fad religion."

"Don't," she said.

"And I know exactly what kind of religious leader I'm going to be. I'll be one of those who takes everybody's money and sleeps with all the women. Just like the Pope, before they did the big cover-up. Ow."

This last, because I'd become too enthused by my own fancy and had started to move in a way that I immediately regretted.

"You deserved that," she said.

I settled back into my pillow and waited for the head-fireworks to subside.

When it was all bearable again I said, "They had to stitch the top of my scalp together like one of those exploding cigars. I can never afford to lose any of my hair after this. I'd be the scariest bald guy you ever saw."

"And probably the luckiest."

"He was aiming square at the middle of my chest. If he'd pulled the trigger then I'd be dead now for sure. But for some reason he switched it to a head shot at the last moment."

"Why would he do that?"

"For certainty, is all I can imagine. If I was wearing a vest, one between the eyes puts an end to any doubt."

"But not this time."

"A gun with a recoil's gonna kick. When you know that's coming, it's hard not to flinch and shoot high. A near-miss at that range isn't so hard to believe."

I'd been brought up on a diet of TV Westerns where the heroes took a bullet crease every other week and thought nothing of it. I didn't think too much of it either. I had a permanently gouged cranial bone and it took major plastic surgery to piece the skin back together so that I wouldn't be Mister Patches the alopecia clown. It didn't result in the facelift I was hoping for, but to this day I'm convinced that my ears are about a quarter of an inch higher than they were before.

Julie said, "Maybe your guardian lwa was giving you protection."

"Yeah," I said. "Forget Simbi the snake god. Mine's Cheetah. Spirit of a chimpanzee in a diaper."

"I'm not joking," she said, and reached down to get something. "Look," she said, "don't be angry . . . " And she laid a small cloth bag on the covers of my bed, like a tiny sack of gold with its neck tied up with a little piece of ribbon. "I put this in your jacket before you went out."

I picked it up. It weighed almost nothing and smelled as if it had been dunked in an inexpensive perfume.

"What is it?" I said.

"It's a gris-gris bag," she said. "Like the one Edwina left with me. I made this one for you the night before, and put it in your pocket when you weren't looking. It's got some of your daughters' hair in it. I took it from their pillows. It probably made no difference to you. But it made me feel better."

I wasn't sure what to say.

"Thanks," I said.

And the gris-gris bag sat there between us, like an

unanswered question.

I said, "What are you planning to do now?"

"Same thing as you," she said. "Sell the house. See what's left over when everything's paid off, try for a smaller place. Maybe somewhere nearer to the hospital."

"Yeah?" I said. This was something new.

"Christopher needs to see his father," she said. "They're saying that Kenny could start coming home at weekends. We'll have to see how it goes."

I remembered to stop myself before nodding and setting off the cranial fireworks again. "Well, what can I say?" I said. "It all sounds like a good idea."

There didn't seem to be much for either of us to say after that. It didn't occur to me until much later that for her to have retrieved the gris-gris bag from my coat pocket, she must have been to visit me when I was either unconscious or too doped-up to register her presence. Maybe that explained the dream of her that I'd had.

We both sat there feeling uncomfortable for a while, then she made a move.

"I need to thank you for everything you've done," she said. "I wish I knew how."

I waved a hand. The one with the hospital band on it.

"Forget it," I said.

She stood there looking awkward.

Then she said, "Look after yourself," and bent over and kissed me quickly on the corner of my mouth.

When she'd gone, I reached around until I found the bed control and then changed the angle a few times in an attempt to get it more comfortable. Julie's visit had taken a lot of the stuffing out of me, but I'd already done more sleeping than felt right in the space of one day. After a while, the Mauritian nurse looked in to check on me.

"How's it going, John?" she said.

"Just seeing what happens when I fiddle around with my knob," I told her, and held up the control for her to see.

I lay there and watched the sunlight pattern slowly creep across my ceiling. That was about as much excitement as I could handle right now.

If I were to turn my head—no small or unambitious project, and one I didn't try too often—I'd be able to look at the flowers and cards on my bedside table. A couple of the cards had come from people I worked with, although most had put their signatures on the big one that had been passed around the department. There was a joint one made on the computer from my cheapskate daughters, and an unsigned one that had come through the mail addressed, in a hand I didn't recognize, to *The Voodoo Cop*.

There was even one from Amy, a pastel thing with a picture of flowers and a copperplate message. You had to look twice to be sure it said *Get Well Soon* and not *In Deepest Sympathy*. The nurse had put it at the front of the pack, and I'd let it stay there. At least she'd signed it properly, and not as Aimee.

I didn't know how that was going to work out. I'd given up trying fathom anything. The only thing I'd learned from life in general is that anything that makes you happy isn't really yours, but is on a lease. They always come and take it from you in the end. The trick is in learning how to let it go.

Bob Lambert had died of his wounds. They'd told me about it on the second day. I thought about him but I tried not to dwell on it.

Any time that I felt low or lacking in entertainment, I'd close my eyes and remember the expression on Dave Corrigan's face as he watched this blood-streaked zombie come stalking up toward him to blind-shoot his captor from more than twenty feet away, *Blam!* leveling and firing without even consciously taking aim, beaning the bocu squarely with less than an inch to spare from his hostage. Take that, Eddie. With Love, The Walking Dead. Others told me afterwards that Dave Corrigan's bowels let go in that moment, and filled his pants so conspicuously that nobody wanted to give him a ride home.

When my spirits got low, I could always enjoy that thought.

I'd have enjoyed it even more, if grinning hadn't made the top of my head hurt so much.

Stephen Gallagher is the author of fifteen novels including Valley of Lights, the Boat House, and Nightmare, With Angel. Read on for a 3-chapter sample from **The Spirit Box**.

THE SPIRIT BOX

Rachel's in trouble. She's a ticking bomb. A couple of co-workers bullied her into stealing a radical new drug from their employer, and now it's lodged inside her. They're watching her like hawks and her time's running out.

John Bishop runs security for the company. As a father who once lost a teenaged daughter to an accidental overdose, his drive to hunt down the thieves and rescue their victim grows more intense with every lost minute. He can never bring his own child back. But he can save someone else's.

Which is fine . . . until his superiors realise that if the swallowed package bursts and Rachel dies, their secrets are kept safe and their problem goes away.

Though Bishop's on the trail, he's an easy man to cut loose and discredit. But now he's Rachel's only hope.

"Gallagher's hardboiled style is pitch-perfect for the tale's grim events, but he leavens it with dislocating moments of powerful emotion that draw the reader irresistibly to the characters. The novel packs a wallop that should make an impact on fans of both suspense and horror fiction."

—Publishers' Weekly

ONE

THE YOUNG black security guard came out of the booth, took the card from my hand, turned it the right way around, and swiped it through the reader. When the barrier started to rise she said, "There you go, Mister Bishop," and handed it back.

"Thanks," I said. My voice sounded scratchy.

The smile that she gave me was professional and courteous. No editorial content in it at all. If my appearance startled her, she didn't show it. If my minute of dumb persistence with the card had aroused her curiosity, she didn't show that either. She went back into the security hut and I drove on into the parking lot.

Macdonald-Stern. The company I'd spent three years helping to set up.

The plant stood in a recently re-zoned piece of open countryside to the south of the airport, out beyond the Vietnamese church. Six years ago, there had been nothing here but woodland. Four years ago the state had put in roads and basic services. All over the USA they built these research parks like cargo cultists laying out airstrips on the beach, hoping to attract the spirits of prosperity. In some areas it didn't work, and you'd see some road named Technology Drive running off into nowhere with nothing along it but weeds and broken fences. Here it was different. Here they laid out the roads and the money came down out of the sky.

I cruised the Lexus around the parking lot. We had parking for a thousand cars in two secure areas. The lots were surrounded by woodland and had video surveillance around the clock. The plant was a short walk away; you could glimpse it from here, looking like a Mayan temple buried deep in the jungle. From the roads outside you couldn't see anything of it at all.

We were a contract house offering analytical service to North Carolina's medical industries. They'd create the interesting-looking molecules and we'd tell them what, if anything, each new substance might be good for. The Mayan temple was one big state-of-the-art lab facility sitting on top of The Spirit Box, an enormous climate-controlled underground vault. In the vault were the test materials belonging to our various clients, kept under conditions of rigid security. Apart from the need to avoid cross-contamination, we based our procedures on the assumption that any one of those client substances might turn out to be the cure for cancer.

Something registered in the corner of my eye, and I felt a sudden shock. Christ, was that *me*? I'd caught sight of myself in the rear view mirror as I was backing into a vacant space. I managed to brake about an inch short of the Taurus in the next slot.

Then I had to take a moment.

When I'd locked the car I walked along the campus-style pathway to the admin building. There I went through the double doors into our entrance hall, and approached the desk.

"Hi," I said to the Security Man behind it.

He said, "Good morning, Mister Bishop."

I looked down at myself. I'd been wearing casual clothes to begin with, and now they were creased and rumpled from a day and a night's wear. There's casual, and there's casual.

I said, "You have to excuse me. I didn't get time to change."

"You look fine to me, sir," the Security Man said. "Can I get you anything?"

"Isn't there somewhere I can get hold of a razor and stuff?"

"You can tell me what you need and I'll have it brought to your office. Or there's a vendor in the second-floor men's room in the west building."

"What kind of things does it have?"

"Razors, toothpaste, shoeshine . . . everything you need except the alibi."

"Thanks," I said. "And while I'm taking care of that, can you call Mickey Cheung in the Spirit Box and tell him I'll be with him in ten minutes?"

He reached for his phone.

"I'll do that," he said.

I said, "Thank you," and set off toward the west building.

I knew I looked bad and I probably looked as if I was hung-over. I caught myself walking unsteadily, and I wouldn't have blamed anyone for thinking I was drunk. But it was sheer physical tiredness. I'd gone around twenty-six hours without sleep and I wasn't about to stop.

I went through the connecting hall and into the west building, where I took the glass elevator up to the second floor. Four other people were along for the ride and not one of them betrayed any sign of having noticed me. They studied the floor, their wristwatches, the view outside.

In the men's room, to the sound of running water, I stood by the washbasins and emptied all of the money out of my pockets and onto the marble. I was able to scrape together enough change for a little vendor pack containing a toothbrush, a comb, floss, breath mints, a sachet of cologne, and a tube of toothpaste that was sized for a doll to use. The men's room lighting was discreet and the mirrors had that gold-tinted glass that makes you look tanned and better than you've any right to, but to my own eyes I still looked like a wreck. I shaved in hot water, washed in cold, combed my hair, cleaned my teeth, did whatever I could to tidy myself up. Someone came in and vanished into one of the toilet cubicles. I never saw who it was. He was still inside there when I left.

Everyone was going about their lives as if nothing remarkable had happened.

Heading back toward the management block, I did my best to walk straight and look steady. The cold water had done something for me. It had dragged me through the sleep barrier and into the new day. Not that the new day was a place I had any great wish to be.

From behind me, I heard, "John!"

I stopped and turned. I saw the boyish figure of Rose Macready. I'd just walked past her.

"Sorry," I said.

"You were walking along in a daze." Then she took a moment to study me more closely. "What happened?"

I wasn't sure what to say, so I just said a lame-sounding, "I had a bad night."

"You should have called me. I could have made it a better one."

"Rose . . ." I began, half-wanting her to be the first one I'd tell, but not even wanting to approach the moment where I told anyone at all.

"I'm teasing you, John," she said. "Come on. What's the order of the day?"

Rose Macready was only one step down from the top job in People Resources. In the old days it would have been called Personnel. She was single, around thirty-five years old, and was the only woman other than Sophie that I'd slept with since I'd been married. Rose and I had agreed to forget it. But I'd found that you don't.

The order of the day?

"I don't know yet," I said.

"Want to meet me for lunch?"

"I think I'll be out," I said.

"Okay," she said, and then as she was turning to walk on, she added, "Talk to me later if you change your mind."

TWO

THE ELEVATOR reached the bottom of the shaft, and I stepped out into the Spirit Box.

Actually, what I entered was the foyer to the vault's Master Control Suite, a subterranean room with the lighting plan of a flight deck and more processing power than a NASA mission. From where I stood I could see into the suite through three walls of glass that were variously angled like the facets on a diamond.

These places always look the same to me. It doesn't matter what they're controlling—a theme park, an Imax cinema, a couple of hundred channels of cable TV—they always have the same hardware, the same feel, the same one guy sitting in the middle of it all reading a newspaper.

Except that today, Mickey Cheung was already on his feet and waiting to buzz me through.

I don't know if it was his black-rimmed glasses or the fact that he spent so much of his working day underground, but almost everything about Mickey made me think of a mole. I reckon that nature had it in mind for him to be small and round, but a twice-weekly workout kept him slim-waisted and chunky like a little Stretch Armstrong.

The doors slid open and as soon as I was through them I said, "You left a message on my service last night. eYou played me a recording of a girl crying. I didn't imagine that, did I? Yes or no?"

But he was staring at me.

"What happened to *you*?" he said.

"Never mind that. You *did* leave me a message?"

"Only after I spent most of the evening trying to get hold of you."

"Well, I'm here now. What was it all about?"

"Security got an anonymous tip-off," he said. "The caller said, if you want to know who's been stealing client samples out of the Spirit Box, take a close look at an employee name of Don Farrow. I checked on Farrow, he's just one of the kids, basically a janitor. I got a master key and looked in his locker. His phone was inside. He had a dozen missed calls and a voicemail waiting. That was the message I played out to you."

"It was a girl's voice."

"I noticed that."

"It sounded like my daughter," I said. "Did you notice *that*?"

He looked at me strangely. "Not to me, it didn't," he said.

"Where's this Don Farrow?" I said. "I want to talk to him."

"Nobody's seen him since the weekend," Mickey said.

"How much substance is there in this?"

"Let me show you."

One of Mickey's assistants took over in the control suite, and I followed him through to the vault itself. The connecting tunnel was narrow-sided and round-ceilinged, and it was lit with an orange-white glow from stripes recessed into the walls. Walking behind Mickey, I found myself looking down at a pale scar on the crown of his head. It made a white L-shaped mark where the hair didn't grow. Mickey's hair was cut short, and it was dark like velvet.

Just like a mole's, in fact.

There was nothing supernatural behind the Vault's nickname. A spirit box was the lockable case in which a

Southern gentleman kept his expensive liquor. Once the name had caught on there were one or two attempts to attach urban legends to it—like a story of a construction worker killed and left buried down there during the excavations, completely untrue—but the name mainly stuck because of the vault's tight security.

It was a clean area with a filtered air supply, just like the environment where they make microchips. Everyone in there had to wear paper suits and masks. A thumbprint reader checked our authorisation and then lasered each of us a wrist tag like a new baby's, barcoded and single-use. We pulled on thin latex gloves and then clipped the tags on over them.

Once through the airlock, we'd have to show our tags for scanning at all the automatic doorways. Otherwise they wouldn't let us through. All movements in the vault were logged on a hard drive and observed by video. Try to cheat the procedure and you'd start a lockdown and a big alert.

We came into the central hub of the vault, a wide corridor with a tight curve to it, and here we moved aside to let one of the suited assistants pass. Her heavy trolley had an electric motor assist. It moved on gray rubber tires and the motor clicked on and off as she maneuvered it.

"Morning, Lucy," Mickey said.

"Hey, Mickey," she said.

She sounded young, and she was a slight figure. I glanced after her as she pulled the logged-out samples toward the lab exit. Seventy-five percent of the people in Mickey's department were the sons and daughters of company employees or contractors. For many of them, it was a first job. For the company it was an unofficial family-friendly policy. For all that this was a high-tech environment theirs was essentially low-grade work, barely a cut above stacking the shelves in a Wal-Mart.

We passed on. In the white light and spacesuits we might have been in some slow-moving science fiction Art Movie. The storage galleries were off to our left, radiating from the corridor like spokes from the hub. There were five levels, all but one of them exactly like this one. We were heading for an internal elevator bank that would take us down to the lowest.

How was I feeling? In turmoil, to be honest with you. On the outside I was moving normally while my gut and all the way up into my chest felt like a tight bag of snakes. Part of me knew beyond all logic that it was Gilly's voice I'd heard in that message. Logic suggested otherwise.

Another of the young interns went by with a trolley of samples for the labs upstairs. Most of them were bright kids, in my limited experience. They were straight enough, but I wouldn't have called any of them committed. Push the wagon, pull the wagon. What kind of a career would you call that?

We rode the elevator down to sub-level five. The elevator car was an odd shape, with a bumper rail at knee height. I could feel a pressure in my head. I don't know if it was real or imagined, but it wasn't pleasant.

This level wasn't quite like the others. It wasn't as bright, it wasn't as stark. It didn't have the same feel as the rest of them, either. When they'd dug right down into the red Carolina dirt they'd taken it all the way to the bedrock, and the bedrock they'd reached wasn't even. So the lowest level of the underground structure was fitted in with the contours of the substrate, which meant that there was less available space and its layout was eccentric. The main corridor wasn't a circle, it was a snake.

The levels above us were like a space station. This was more like a space station's crypt. Bare concrete, sealed. Bulkhead lighting. A painted floor. Of all the levels, this was the least-used. There was almost nothing down here but the old Russian stuff.

Lights flickered on as we stepped out of the elevator. They'd sensed our presence, and they'd power-down after we'd quit the area. Mickey knew where he was going, and led me around a couple of turns and into the second of three parallel galleries.

"Something here you need to see," he said.

The ceiling was low and the walls had a slight kink to them, so that the far end of the chamber ran on just out of sight. There had to be a thousand or more client samples on the shelves in this one gallery. They were all in packaging that was basic and low-tech. I saw a varied selection of scruffy boxes and jars, each item placed on its weight-sensitive pedestal and underlit like installation art. I could see at least one brown-paper parcel that had been vacuum-sealed into a thick plastic envelope, string and address labels and all.

"You're looking at the Soviet fire sale collection," Mickey Cheung said. "When it came to us, it arrived in fifty crates without a scrap of documentation. Our deal with the client is that we work on it at cheap rate when there's slack time in the labs. Barely two per cent's been touched, and nothing in that's been useful."

We walked down the gallery, and Mickey said, "Each individual sample is logged with a number and stands on a pressure pad recording its mass. The theory is that if any part of any sample gets removed without authorisation, it shows up. I've got five samples down here that defied the laws of physics and got bigger. We got variations of up to half a gram over recorded weight. That's too much of an increase for either oxidation or moisture to account for."

We stopped before the samples. There were five different jars, all with screw-on lids, and I could see that each had been topped up with a white powder that didn't quite match the contents of any of them. Something had spilled. I wiped a gloved finger across the shelf by the base of the nearest jar, and it left a clean mark.

"Talcum powder?" I said.

"At a guess," Mickey said.

"Anything here that's high-value?"

"The chemicals are probably worth less than the talcum powder," He said. "You'd hear rumors about the kind of things the Russians were working on, but we've yet to find anything startling to back them up. I reckon it was mostly just Cold War propaganda. Bear in mind that all this stuff came from the labs that couldn't hack it in the free market. All the promising research found commercial sponsors."

"So the chances of pulling out a golden ticket are pretty slim."

"I'm not saying there's no possible chance of finding the chemical basis of a brand-new zillion-dollar product somewhere in here. The problem is that you're looking at everything from bug spray to voodoo juice, and nobody knows which is which."

"Voodoo juice?"

"Zombie cucumber from the parapsychology labs in Krasnodar. Imagine anyone being prepared to shell out a quarter of a mill for *that*."

"So why pick on these to steal?"

"Because if you look around, you can see that this is the only area the cameras don't cover."

We were finished, here. He'd made his point and there was nothing more of use that we could do. I was glad to get out.

As we were going back up in the elevator, I said to Mickey, "How would Don Farrow get the stuff out of the vault?"

"He wouldn't. Don Farrow's never had access down here. So we're probably talking about a team."

"That still leaves the problem of getting the stuff through the searches."

He sucked in and blew out a faintly exasperated breath, and the sides of his mask moved with the pressure.

"Well," he said, "you've seen the procedure. You strip to walk in, you strip to walk out. My guess is that ingestion or body cavity would be the only ways to go."

"You mean, swallow it?"

"Or stick it where the sun don't often shine. Personally, I'd swallow it. I wouldn't care to have a workmate stroll around the corner and find me in mid-insertion. There's no easy quip for an occasion such as that."

There was nothing more to see or say, so we returned to the surface. I was finding it hard to get my breath so I pulled my mask off in the elevator. I was aware of Mickey watching me. Studying me, even. I didn't look up or meet his eyes.

"Rough night last night?" he said after a while.

"May you never know," I said.

THREE

L ET ME just take you back to the day before.
With luck it'll explain everything. Why I was in the
state that I was in, and why I went on to do what I did.

She stood at the top of the stairs and called down to
me, "Daddy, I've done something stupid."

And that really was the beginning of it.

I looked up from the box that I was packing. She was at
the top of the big open-plan stairway that came down from
the bedroom level and right into the living area. It was a
huge house, the kind they mean when they talk about a
place to die for. And rented, of course. We'd been in it for
most of the three years. Gillian was holding the handrail
and looking scared.

"No kidding," I said testily. "What now?"

There was a lot still to be done, and she hadn't been of
much help so far. She'd been moody and obstructive in the
way that only a fifteen-year-old can. My immediate guess
was that she'd been kicking at the doors or the furniture,
taking out her resentment on the fabric of the place, and
now she was worried because something had been
damaged.

"Seriously," she said.

I can't tell you if she took a mis-step then or if her legs
just gave out, but I could see her waver and then her foot
missed the stair. Her heel clipped the riser and she sat
down heavily, all at once. One hand was still holding the
rail and she seemed to have no coordination. She slipped
down onto the second stair and looked for a moment as if
she might lose her grip and slide all the way.

I've no memory of laying down whatever I was holding, or of crossing the room. All I remember is that in an instant I was up there with her, steadying her onto the third step down. She let go of the handrail and she held onto my arm tightly.

"What have you done?" I said. A pallor had washed out her tan, and I could see the blue of the veins through her skin. Her touch was cold and very damp. Her hand on my arm seemed small.

"I took some pills," she said.

"What pills?" I said. "Where?"

"The ones you told me to clear out of the bathroom cabinet."

I tried to make it all compute. But it just wouldn't go. Pills. Bathroom cabinet. She'd done *what*? I tried to grasp the sense of it, the scale. But I was utterly unprepared.

"Oh, Jesus," I said.

I disengaged myself and left her there, and I went through the master bedroom to the bathroom. The bedroom had its own deck overlooking the lake, and a loft area which I'd been using as an office. The bathroom was carpeted, tiled, marbled, jacuzzied. The lighting alone would be enough to make you feel like you'd made it, that to live in a place like this you had to be up there with the rich. She'd left the lights switched on. The hidden fan was running.

The cabinet was directly above the basin. Its doors were wide open and the middle shelf had been swept clear of bottles and containers. As far as I could remember there should have been eight or a dozen of these, mostly over-the-counter remedies that had been bought as needed and then kept in case they'd ever be needed again.

All that remained on the shelf was the floss and the toothpaste, pushed over to one side. Most of the containers lay in the basin below, their childproof caps off. I sorted out odd ones at random, and shook them. Only one or two still had tablets inside. The rest were empty.

There were more medicines here than I could remember buying, and a few empty blister packs as well. Some we'd brought out with us from England. Others had the labels of various American drugstores. I'd never really kept track.

She surely couldn't have taken *all* of them. Could she? But if she hadn't, where were they?

I went back. She was still on the third stair down. She was hunched forward with her arms wrapped around her middle and her head almost on her knees.

I sat beside her and showed her the plastic bottle in my hand. It was a twenty-five capsule pack of painkillers and there was one lone caplet rattling around inside it.

"Where's the rest of these?" I said.

"Don't shout at me," she said.

I wasn't shouting. Or I didn't think I was. But I needed her to feel some of the urgency that was beginning to overwhelm me. I was thinking that I wanted her to see it and remember it so that this would never, ever happen again.

I said, "I'm just trying to work out what you did."

She wiped her eyes with her sleeve, and obviously not for the first time. They were teary and red and sore.

"I told you," she said.

"You didn't tell me how many."

I waited.

"Oh, God," I said. "You didn't really take them all."

"I'm sorry," she said miserably.

Phone. Ambulance.

I tried to stand, and she clung onto me.

"No," she said.

I was about to say something sharp when I realized that she wasn't trying to prevent me from getting to a phone. She just didn't want me to leave her alone on the stairs again. She wasn't letting go.

"Come on," I said. "Let's get you downstairs. Stand up."

"I can't."

"I'll help you."

She wasn't exaggerating. I genuinely don't think she had the strength to stand up unaided. I had to take most of her weight as I walked her down the stairs while she moved her legs like a puppet does, brushing the ground and not really walking at all. We couldn't move anywhere near as fast as I would have liked.

"I want to go to a hospital," she said.

"I know."

"I want to go now."

"I'll call an ambulance."

Down the stairs, one at a time, me taking the weight, both of us moving in slow motion.

"I feel awful," she said.

"Well," I said, "it was a stupid thing to do."

I got her down to the living room couch, where she rolled onto her side and curled up like a sick animal.

"Try to bring some of them back, Gilly," I said.

"No," she moaned.

"Put your fingers down your throat. If you don't do it, I'll have to."

First aid? I had no idea. Who does? They used to tell you to make a child drink salt water to trigger the vomit reflex. Now they say don't, because of saline poisoning. Throwing up helps. Or makes it worse. It all depends.

There had never been any time in my life when I needed help more.

My phone was out in the car so I picked up the house

phone, and it was dead.

Of course it was. I don't know why I was surprised. I'd arranged disconnection myself, less than a week ago. They'd asked me to pick a time and I'd said, off the top of my head, Oh, why don't we make it ten o'clock. I'd been assuming that we'd be done and out by then.

In spite of this I dialed 911 anyway, and of course nothing happened, and so then like an idiot I dialed it again, and then I slammed down the receiver ran out to the Lexus.

The Spirit Box ©Stephen Gallagher The Brooligan Press
284pp ISBN 9780995797376

THE SEBASTIAN BECKER NOVELS

Chancery lunatics were people of wealth or property whose fortunes were at risk from their madness. Those deemed unfit to manage their affairs had them taken over by lawyers of the Crown, known as the Masters of Lunacy. It was Sebastian's employer, the Lord Chancellor's Visitor, who would decide their fate. Though the office was intended to be a benevolent one, many saw him as an enemy to be outwitted or deceived, even to the extent of concealing criminal insanity.

It was for such cases that the Visitor had engaged Sebastian. His job was to seek out the cunning dissembler, the dangerous madman whose resources might otherwise make him untouchable. Rank and the social order gave such people protection. A former British police detective and one-time Pinkerton man, Sebastian had been engaged to work 'off the books' in exposing their misdeeds. His modest salary was paid out of the department's budget. He remained a shadowy figure, an investigator with no public profile.

THE KINGDOM OF BONES

After prizefighter-turned-stage manager Tom Sayers is wrongly accused in the slayings of pauper children, he disappears into a twilight world of music halls and temporary boxing booths. While Sayers pursues the elusive actress Louise Porter, the tireless Detective Inspector Sebastian Becker pursues him. This brilliantly macabre mystery begins in the lively parks of Philadelphia in 1903, then winds its way from England's provincial playhouses and London's mighty Lyceum Theatre to the high society of a transforming American South—and the alleyways, back stages, and houses of ill repute in between.

"Vividly set in England and America during the booming industrial era of the late 19th and early 20th centuries, this stylish thriller conjures a perfect demon to symbolize the age and its appetites"
—New York Times

THE BEDLAM DETECTIVE

...finds Becker serving as Special Investigator to the Masters of Lunacy in the case of a man whose travellers' tales of dinosaurs and monsters are matched by a series of slaughters on his private estate. An inventor and industrialist made rich by his weapons patents, Sir Owain Lancaster is haunted by the tragic outcome of an ill-judged Amazon expedition in which his entire party was killed. When local women are found slain on his land, he claims that the same dark Lost-World forces have followed him home.

"A rare literary masterpiece for the lovers of historical crime fiction."
—MysteryTribune

THE AUTHENTIC WILLIAM JAMES

As the Special Investigator to the Lord Chancellor's Visitor in Lunacy, Sebastian Becker delivers justice to those dangerous madmen whose fortunes might otherwise place them above the law. But in William James he faces a different challenge; to prove a man sane, so that he may hang. Did the reluctant showman really burn down a crowded pavilion with the audience inside? And if not, why is this British sideshow cowboy so determined to shoulder the blame?

"It's a blinding novel... the acerbic wit, the brilliant dialogue—the sheer spot-on elegance of the writing: the plot turns, the pin sharp beats. Always authoritative and convincing, never showy. Magnificently realised characters in a living breathing world . . . Absolutely stunning"
—Stephen Volk
(Ghostwatch, Gothic, Afterlife)

"Gallagher gives Sebastian Becker another puzzle worthy of his quirky sleuth's acumen in this outstanding third pre-WW1 mystery"
—Publishers Weekly starred review

CPSIA information can be obtained
at www.ICGtesting.com
Printed in the USA
LVHW011730180219
607899LV00003B/779/P

9 780995 797383